— *A Bitter* —
BOUQUET

A Tea & Sympathy Mystery

BOOK 4

J. NEW

A Bitter Bouquet
A Tea & Sympathy Mystery
Book 4

Copyright © J. New 2021

Cover design: J. New.
Interior formatting: Alt 19 Creative

OTHER BOOKS BY J. NEW

The Yellow Cottage Vintage Mysteries in order:
The Yellow Cottage Mystery (Free)
An Accidental Murder
The Curse of Arundel Hall
A Clerical Error
The Riviera Affair
A Double Life

The Finch & Fischer Mysteries in order:
Decked in the Hall
Death at the Duck Pond
Battered to Death

Tea & Sympathy Mysteries in order:
Tea & Sympathy
A Deadly Solution
Tiffin & Tragedy
A Bitter Bouquet

Chapter One

LILLY TWEED STOOD outside her shop, The Tea Emporium, in the small market town of Plumpton Mallet, with her hands on her hips and her head tilted as she surveyed with a critical eye the colourful display she had been tinkering with all morning. As usual, it comprised her bicycle with its sturdy wicker basket, but rather than the plethora of brightly coloured flowing plants she usually displayed throughout the spring and summer months, the imminent onset of autumn meant an entirely different aesthetic.

Now, the brightly coloured bicycle was surrounded with pumpkins and squash in various shades, ranging from pale cream to bright orange. The larger ones were positioned on the ground next to the front and rear wheels, while the smaller ones she'd stuffed inside the basket along with decorative leaves, dried flowers, and burlap.

"Yes, I think that will do nicely," she said with a nod, glancing at the window behind the display where Earl Grey, the former beat up old stray now official shop cat, was watching her movements with interest.

"What do you think, Earl?" she asked him through the glass. The cat, sensing the entertainment was over, gave her a grandiose look typical of felines everywhere, swished his tail and climbed back into his own basket. Moments later, with a paw over his nose, he was asleep. Lilly smiled. "I'll just assume you approve," she said, making her way back inside, only pausing to collect the post from the agony aunt box.

"Any letters today?" Stacey, her bubbly American assistant, asked.

"Just the one," she replied, opening it. It was from an elderly, housebound local woman who was looking for something that would relieve her gout. Her daughter-in-law had suggested tea might help, so she was writing to Lilly in the hope she could assist. She could. There were three teas she stocked, which could help lower uric acid levels. The first a Hibiscus blend, the second a green tea with a high antioxidant concentration, which would help reduce the joint inflammation and swelling. The third a cherry and nettle blend. She'd pack up some free samples of each and send them to her to try. Making her way behind the counter where Stacey was restocking the drawers of the apothecary cabinet with tea samples, she weighed them out.

The Tea Emporium was one of the oldest buildings in Plumpton Mallet and had been built originally as a chemist. Wanting to keep the decor as authentic as possible, Lilly now used the large, old oak cabinet to house her teas. With its myriad drawers with half moon brass handles, it was her favourite piece in the entire shop.

"Just the one letter?" Stacey said. "You haven't had very many this week compared to usual."

"Well, I suppose technically it's still summer. I think the letters will pick up again once the holiday season is over."

"So, you admit it's way too early to whip out the pumpkins?" Stacey asked, with an enormous grin splitting her face from ear to ear. She'd been teasing Lilly all morning about being the first business in the town to start with the autumn decor. Most of the other shops still had their summer displays up, and Stacey couldn't believe Lilly was already thinking about the latter part of the year. She'd explained to her boss that people in America didn't put up fall displays until summer was well and truly over, and even then it wasn't until October that the decorations were in full swing.

Lilly shrugged. "Well, here in Britain we celebrate the Harvest Festival toward the end of September. I'm just two or three weeks early, that's all."

Stacey frowned. "What's that?"

"It's giving thanks for successful harvests on the Sunday nearest to the harvest moon, the full moon closest to the autumn equinox. It's been going since pagan times, although obviously it didn't start in the churches that came in the late 1800s. Nowadays, the churches are decorated with baskets of fruit and food, and hymns sung and prayers said. It was a big thing when I was in school, that's why I remember the dates so clearly."

"Wow, sounds great. I didn't know about it."

"Also, I think planning this wedding has made me want a change of decor. The bride has chosen quite a few autumn colours."

Lilly had been asked to cater for a local wedding, and it delighted her to be helping. The catering would mean more customers for her and a chance for the business to branch out into larger events. She'd been going over her tea inventory and ordering speciality teas to go with the wedding theme for the last few weeks. So far, she'd chosen Orange Blossom White, Hibiscus Superflower and Raspberry Rose Hibiscus, as well as a more traditional red tea with cinnamon. She'd also designed special signature cocktails to be served in the teacups and saucers, the bride having chosen a vintage high tea theme for her nuptials. These included Rosemary Greyhound, Blackberry and Honeysuckle Spritz, Pink Gin Fizz, and Tipsy Hibiscus with Green Tea. Naturally, she and Stacey had had a lot of fun tasting and testing.

As things had progressed, the bride had asked Lilly to take on more and more of the planning and she'd accepted the role gladly. She'd become involved with both the table decorations and the flowers.

As Lilly and Stacey poured over various tea sets, Lilly intended to purchase as a wedding gift for the happy couple, Bethany Roman entered the shop, a large three-ring binder under her arm and a serious look on her face.

"Oh, boy," Stacey muttered, catching Lilly's eye and smirking. "Here we go..."

*L*ILLY GAVE HER a wink in reply, then plastered on a smile to greet their visitor.

"Good day, ladies," Bethany called out, strutting across the shop floor to greet them.

"Hello, Bethany. I see you have the wedding book with you." Lilly replied.

"And lunch. It's afternoon now, Lilly. I thought I'd save you the trouble of coming over." Bethany said, putting two take away bags on the counter.

"Oh, that's great. Thanks." Stacey said, grabbing a bag and peering inside.

"That's very kind of you," Lilly said.

Bethany was the owner of the local cafe where Stacey and Lilly regularly bought their lunch. It was only a few doors down from The Tea Emporium, and besides the food being top-notch and delicious, it was also reasonably priced. When Lilly was approached to do the catering for the wedding, she'd immediately thought of bringing Bethany on board, having received one of her fliers through The Tea Emporium door a couple of weeks prior advertising the catering side for various celebrations, and seen a beautiful wedding cake displayed in the window of her cafe. It was a job the woman was more than willing to do.

However, Lilly hadn't realised just how exacting Bethany would be with her planning. She was absolutely meticulous and had timed everything down to the last minute. The sections in her binder detailed every little thing. From the aperitifs to the appetisers. The exact time the wedding cake would be brought out and when it would be cut. It even included the step-by-step recipes for the cocktails Lilly had designed. Not only that, she had included drawings of where the food would be placed and who would serve what. The position of the flower vases and what blooms they would contain. She'd even noted the length the flower stems had to be trimmed to. Lilly thought the whole thing was over the top, and because of the very nature of people unlikely to proceed in such a regimented fashion, but she admired Bethany's attention to the fine detail.

"You have your lunch, Stacey," Lilly said. "I hadn't realised how late it was."

Stacey thanked them both, and with Earl in tow hoping for a scrap of whatever the delicious smelling bag contained, disappeared upstairs to her flat.

"Have a told you how much I like that American girl?" Bethany said, putting the large binder on the counter.

"I think you've mentioned it once or twice," Lilly replied, laughing. "And I agree wholeheartedly. It was a good day when she walked into my shop and asked for a job. Mind you, her autumn term will start soon, so you won't be seeing much of her after the wedding is over."

"Perhaps you should consider a second employee?"

"You're probably right. Let me know if you hear of anyone looking for a job, would you? Now, what have you got for me?"

Bethany opened to a page and tapped it with a pale pink varnished fingernail. "Yasemin has sent me an email. I've now got the final food menu from her," she said. "She's decided to scrap the whole idea of blending Turkish and English foods."

"Really? I thought she loved that idea?"

Lilly had wondered how Bethany had taken the news. She knew the woman had stayed up several nights planning the perfect combination of two distinct types of food, and had even brought samples over to Lilly, which she'd loved. She looked at the page Bethany was showing and found stunning examples of old, classic place settings and elaborate fancies. Whatever Yasemin wanted, she had full confidence in Bethany's ability to achieve it.

"She's decided to go with the full English vintage theme. Few of her family RSVP'd sadly. I think originally she wanted to both pay homage to her heritage and appease her family, but since hardly any of them are bothering to make the trip from Turkey, she's decided to stick with what she wanted in the first place."

"Well, good for her. A bride should have the wedding she wants and if she wants English vintage, then that's what we will do."

"From what I understand, it was her mother who was pressuring her for the Turkish element, but now she's not attending," Bethany said.

"Her own mother isn't coming?" Lilly asked in surprise.

"She said she came to the first one and that should have been it. She's not prepared to be present at this one," Bethany said, shaking her head. "Yasemin told me there's a strong feeling in her family about her remarrying."

"Ah, I forgot she was divorced. Isn't her ex-husband attending?"

"He is. He's good friends with the groom, apparently. I'm not sure how all the unique personalities and relationships work, but I understand the split was amicable."

"I'm divorced myself," Lilly said. "But amicable split or not, I can't imagine I'd ever want to invite my ex-husband to my second wedding."

"Well no, me neither, truth be told. But it's not really any of our business. What is our business is what these guests are going to be eating and drinking at this fabulous vintage wedding. I can't thank you and Stacey enough for bringing me on board, Lilly. Things have been a little slow at the cafe lately."

"Oh? I must say I'm surprised to hear that. Your food is superb. I'm astonished you don't have a queue of customers snaking around the market square every day," Lilly said. "Well, let's see what we can get done today. We've still got a lot of details to work out before the big day."

Bethany nodded and with a special vintage blend of tea Lilly made just for them, the two women rolled up their sleeves to continue with their plans.

Originally, Lilly had been hired for her teas, cocktails and finding a sub-contractor for the catering, but later the bride had asked if she could also take on the decorating. She'd agreed throwing herself into the research immediately and was enjoying the challenge immensely. The two women worked tirelessly for an hour while fortifying themselves with the food Bethany had brought.

"Right," Bethany said, shutting her folder. "I think that's all we can do for today. I have a cafe to get back to. Even though we're not too busy at the moment, there's always something that needs doing. We work well together, Lilly. This wedding should go off without a hitch. Well, apart from the main one," she laughed, waving goodbye and exiting the shop.

Stacey reappeared a moment later, Earl at her side. He looked at Lilly and gave a loud and demanding meow.

"Is that your way of telling me it's time to feed you, too, Mr Grey?"

"I'll do it. I think he's annoyed that he didn't get any of my sandwich." Stacey said, retreating to the back room kitchen and calling the cat, who bolted in her direction as soon as he heard the fridge door open.

They spent the rest of the afternoon assisting regular customers and tourists to choose the perfect tea for their various ailments or gifts for loved ones, and before Lilly knew, it was time to close. She moved the autumnal display from the bicycle to the window, and with Stacey already upstairs in her flat, put Earl, happily snuggled in his carrier, into the basket, locked the door and cycled home. Her mind a whirl of new ideas for the wedding.

Chapter Two

$\mathcal{I}$T WAS ANOTHER day closer to the wedding, and Lilly was out and about in town with the bride-to-be, Yasemin Yildiz, doing some decor shopping.

"You're superb at this, Lilly," Yasemin said as the two women entered a nearby antique shop. Their arms already laden with bags from their day so far. Now they were trying to find the perfect table for the Bride and Groom's lover's seat at the reception.

"I'm glad you think so," Lilly said. "I enjoy it."

"I know this job wasn't what I originally hired you for, but Esen, my maid-of-honour, isn't flying in from Turkey until two days before the wedding, so I've been having to do most of the planning myself. It's been exhausting. Of course, Edmund's cousins have tried to help, but they are so busy."

"Do you know, I think I may have met your husband before," Lilly said. "He's a local man, isn't he?"

"From London actually, but he comes here often as he has a cousin in the area, Bruce. It is him who is letting us use his property for the ceremony and the reception. It's a beautiful old estate, and I fell in love with it the first time I visited with Edmund on holiday. I knew immediately it was where I wanted us to get married. You've probably met Edmund, though. He was the one who told me about your shop and I insisted we go immediately. You were away at the time, I think?"

"Yes, I was visiting friends on the coast."

Edmund, Yasemin's fiancé, was a property investor and from the little Lilly understood, travelled a lot with his business.

"How did the two of you meet? Was it through Edmund's job?" she asked, curious, as the two of them browsed through the antique furniture.

Yasemin covered her face.

"Oh, I so hate to tell this story, I get so many strange looks."

"Honestly, you don't have to tell me if you're not comfortable. But I certainly won't judge. I was just interested. In my former job as an agony aunt, I brought quite a few couples together. I like happy endings."

"My ex-husband introduced us. It sounds quite bizarre, I know, but there was nothing going on between Edmund and me when Mirac and I were married. You see, they were at university together and have remained good friends ever since. Edmund was interested in investing in a property that Mirac knew a lot about, so turned to him for advice. They arranged to meet and with nothing better for me to do that day, I came along with Mirac. You must understand, Mirac and I were practically divorced when he introduced us. He said we would make a charming couple. Very awkward at the time," she finished, blushing furiously.

"Mirac did? While the two of you were still married?" Lilly asked, astonished despite herself.

Yasemin nodded. "More or less. Mirac and I... well, we never actually wanted to get married in the first place. It wasn't an arranged marriage, but there was a lot of family pressure on both sides, as our parents were friends. Before we knew it, we were husband and wife, more to keep the peace than anything else, but we both came to regret it. We'd been talking about divorcing for some time before I met Edmund."

"So, you and Edmund hit it off and Mirac, what, just bowed out?" Lilly asked, then bit her lip, embarrassed. "I'm so sorry. That was far too nosy, wasn't it? You don't have to tell me anything else."

Yasemin smiled. "It's fine, honestly. No, that's not how it happened. I only met Edmund that one time. Then Mirac and I finally got divorced. About a year later, my mother and I planned a trip to London and Mirac kindly reached out to Edmund on our behalf. Edmund gave us a personal tour of the city and we stayed in touch after that. He visited Turkey a few times also to see Mirac. As Mirac and I socialise in the same circles, it was inevitable that we would meet, and we did so quite frequently. Eventually, I obtained a job in London and, as Edmund was the only person I knew there to begin with, we met up a few times. We got to know one another quite well after that and things progressed. Much to my mother's dismay, unfortunately. She was happy for him to be our guide during the holiday, but certainly nothing more. However, you can't choose who you fall in love with, can you? She'll come round eventually when she sees how happy we are. Especially if there are grandchildren involved."

"I'm happy things have worked out so well for you both," Lilly said. "And Mirac is attending the wedding?"

"Yes, he is Edmund's best man. It may sound strange to you, but we have a very good relationship. We are old family friends and have known each other since we were children. And of course he's close to Edmund."

Lilly noticed Yasemin brightened up every time she mentioned her fiancé. It was obvious she was very much in love with him. Lilly found she also had the utmost respect for Mirac. It wasn't every day you found an ex-husband who was strong or mature enough to let his wife go in order for her to find true love.

"I don't find it strange at all. I admire Mirac for being able to let you move forward with your life. You and Edmund became friends before being engaged, too. I think that's a good basis for a long and happy marriage, actually."

"Thank you, Lilly. I do too. Although Mirac and I were also friends, we were more like brother and sister. My love for Edmund is completely different."

"Oh, look at this table, Yasemin," Lilly said, winding her way through the floor of the shop to the far corner. It was a charming oblong shape in sturdy oak, with an intricate design of doves entwined with hearts and roses down the legs. It was the perfect size for the couple and Lilly loved it immediately. The price was well within their budget due to slight damage on the bottom of one of the legs, but Lilly knew she could easily repair it if Yasemin thought it was suitable.

"Oh, it's absolutely perfect," Yasemin breathed in delight. "And it will look beautiful in our home after the wedding is over. Let me just call Edmund's cousin. She insisted on making our personal place settings as a wedding gift. I just want to make sure the table size is right for what she has planned."

While Yasemin stepped aside to make her call, Lilly examined the table more closely. It really was a beautifully proportioned piece, and the carvings would coordinate with any place settings chosen.

While Lilly couldn't hear what was being said on the other end of the phone, she could suddenly make out an angry shrieking. There was also a very disappointed look on Yasemin's face.

"I know, Rachel... it's fine. Don't worry about it. I'm sure I can work something out myself," she said, ending the call.

"Oh, dear. What's happened?" Lilly asked.

"It's Rachel," Yasemin said, tearfully. "I'm under the distinct impression she doesn't like me very much. Apparently she's decided not to make the place settings any more. She's too busy."

Lilly really felt for the poor girl. It appeared as though one by one people were letting her down and she was having to plan her wedding on her own.

"She's one of Edmund's cousins?"

"One of many. She's come up from London early to help with the wedding. Although I don't think she's actually done anything except keep Edmund unnecessarily busy. A part of me wonders if she's just come to Plumpton Mallet to make things difficult." Yasemin sighed. "I'm sorry, that sounds very petty, doesn't it? I'm sure she means well..."

Lilly could tell the girl was getting more and more distressed. With the disappointments so far, she needed someone in her corner and Lilly was more than happy to lend a hand.

"I have plenty of place settings at my shop, Yasemin. I'm sure I'll have something that will be perfect for the two of you and will compliment the settings for the rest of the guests."

Yasemin smiled brightly and breathed a huge sigh of relief.

"Really? Thank you so much, Lilly. You're a life saver."

Lilly nodded, wondering why Edmund's cousin had suddenly changed her mind. It was one thing to be busy with family or work, but according to Yasemin, Rachel had travelled up from London specifically to assist with the planning. What had happened to make her back out so late in the day?

"Since you're using my place settings, you can get this table. I know it will all look very elegant together. I'll ask them to deliver it to the shop and I'll mend it in time for your special day."

"Oh, thank you so much, Lilly," Yasemin said.

Lilly knew the shop owner, and he said he'd ask his assistant to deliver it to Lilly later the same day. On the return journey to The Tea Emporium, the two women browsed a few more shops and found some other trinkets to use for decoration and Yasemin was thrilled. The phone call with Rachel seemingly forgotten.

*B*ACK AT THE shop, Lilly showed her a selection of the place settings available. She had a personal favourite, but rather than making suggestions, she let Yasemin browse and pick the one that appealed to her the most.

"They're all wonderful, but I think this one is the best for the vintage theme and to go with the rest of the table settings."

She'd chosen a plain white with an ornate gold filigree design around the rim. It was the ideal accompaniment to the plain white with single gold lined rim that was being used for the rest of the guests.

"That's the one I would have chosen myself," Lilly said. "And I have everything you need in stock, so there's no need to order anything. In terms of silverware, what do you think of these?" She showed Yasemin a Victorian-era reproduction knife and fork with a stylised heart engraved on the handle.

"Oh, yes. These are exactly what I was looking for. Well done, Lilly."

With the settings chosen. Yasemin thanked Lilly for all her help and left with a noticeable spring in her step.

"Lilly," Stacey said, poking her head round the door of the storeroom. "There's a guy here with a table for you."

"Oh, excellent. It's for the wedding. Can you mind the shop while I deal with it?"

Ten minutes later, the table was in situ in Lilly's work space and Stacey was leaning against the storeroom door frame, where she could keep an eye on the shop and chat to Lilly at the same time.

"That's gorgeous. Needs a bit of work though."

"It does, but nothing a bit of wood filler and some acrylics can't fix. I was also thinking of applying some gold leaf to pick out a couple of the carved hearts. What do you think?"

"Great idea!" Stacey said, full of enthusiasm. "Can I help? I learned a bit from my mom, and what I don't know you can teach me."

"Of course. I'd be grateful for the help considering we've not got much time before the wedding day."

When the shop had closed for the day, Lilly and Stacey rolled up their sleeves and got to work. Once the wood filler was set hard, Stacey gently sanded it down while Lilly started on the gold leaf. Carefully painting size on the area to be covered, she waited until it was tacky then applied the thin sheets of faux gold leaf, rubbing it with a soft cloth so it stuck, then gently brushing the excess away with a large artist brush into a waiting bowl.

With the filler now ready for painting, Lilly mixed several tubes of acrylic paint, making sure she had matching colours for both the base and the grain, then set about duplicating the patterns. By the time she had finished, you couldn't tell where the missing piece had been.

"That looks amazing," Stacey said. "You can't even see where it was broken, and the gold is perfect. It will look great with the tableware."

"All we need to do now is give it a polish with beeswax and it will be ready to move to the venue."

She sent Yasemin a quick text to tell her the table could be picked up in the morning, and received a reply almost immediately, telling her one of Edmund's cousins would be there. Lilly hoped this cousin would be more reliable than the previous one.

With the shop cleaned up ready for the next day, Lilly said goodbye to Stacey and Earl, who was going to spend the night upstairs in the flat with Stacey, locked up and walked down to Bethany's cafe. The door was locked, but she could see a light inside, so knocked and waited for her to open the door.

"Lilly, I didn't expect to see you again today. Is everything all right?"

"Everything's fine. Just a couple of updates for you. I thought I'd pop in and tell you on my way home. I'm also hoping you've got some of that vegetable quiche and Mediterranean pasta left? I'm too tired to cook."

"I have indeed. I'll pack it up for you while you tell me what's been happening."

Lilly brought Bethany up to date regarding the lover's table and new place settings. When she explained about Yasemin being let down at the last minute by one of Edmund's cousins, Bethany tutted and shook her head.

"Poor girl. Getting married is stressful enough without having to contend with inconsiderate relatives. The cousin sounds like a dreadful person. But I'm sure you and I can make sure everything goes to plan for them both."

Lilly agreed. It was the least they could do.

Chapter Three

*T*HE NEXT EVENING, after a hectic day at the shop, Lilly got in her car and drove to meet Archie at one of his favourite pubs for an early dinner. He'd insisted on it being his treat as they hadn't seen one another for a gossip and a catch up in a while.

Lilly was glad of the excuse to stop thinking about wedding plans, even if it was just for a few hours. She'd somehow found herself agreeing to also, take on the flowers for the bride, her bridesmaids, and the buttonholes for the men. She'd had to call three different florists before she found one who stocked the flowers Yasemin had requested. After several conversations and emails back and forth containing potential images, they eventually confirmed designs for it all, and the florist promised Lilly everything would be delivered to the venue on the morning of the wedding.

Lilly was never more grateful or relieved that she had Stacey at the shop to help the customers while she herself was either on the phone, out shopping or liaising with Bethany. She was so caught up in the wedding plans she was having nightmares about it. Just the night before, she'd dreamed Edmund's cousins had all stood up and objected right before the couple said I do. Thank goodness Archie had persisted in his requests to meet for dinner.

Although it was still technically summer, there was a distinct chill in the early evening air, so they had agreed to meet in the pub's snug. When she entered, she found Archie at a table in the corner, a pint of best bitter next to him, perusing the latest edition of The Plumpton Mallet Gazette.

"Good evening, Mr Brown," she said, plonking herself on the seat opposite with a groan.

"Miss Tweed," he replied, doffing an imaginary hat with a grin. "Now, what can I get you to drink, my dear? You look as though you need something a little stronger than fruit juice."

"I do. I'm driving so I'll just have the one. Make it a large gin and tonic please, Archie, the meal will soak up the alcohol before it's time for me to leave. You can order the food while you're there too, if you want? I'm happy to have whatever you choose. My brain is officially on strike and refuses to make any more decisions."

Archie went to the bar and brought back an artisan gin the colour of pale pink roses, with various botanicals floating in the liquid. Lilly took a sip and smiled appreciatively.

"That's just perfect, Archie. Thank you. So how have you been? How's life at the paper?"

"Better," he said.

"Really? I was expecting you to huff and groan like you normally do when I ask that question. So what's changed?"

"Abigail is on holiday."

Lilly laughed. "Yes, I suppose that would make for a more peaceful workplace."

"Don't get me wrong, she's really making an effort to get on with people now, but she just never shuts up. You know me and inane chatter. It drives me balmy. I tell you, if talking was an Olympic sport, Abigail would be on the gold podium every time."

"So, how is the agony aunt column doing under her charge?"

"It's died a death, unfortunately. It's part of the reason she's taking a break. Between you, me, and the gatepost, I very much doubt she'll have a job when she gets back. Personally, I think she needs to find a different vocation altogether. She's really appalling at giving advice."

"Where has she gone on holiday?"

Archie shook his head. "She's visiting family, by all accounts. I'm not sure where, though."

Poor Abigail, Lilly thought. They'd never really got on, but she didn't want her to be sacked from her job. Abigail had once told her it was the only thing she had and the reason she had a roof over her head. She idly wondered what she would do when she returned. *If* she returned, she amended.

"I heard Bonnie passed all her exams with flying colours," she said, changing the subject.

"Indeed. She's now a fully fledged detective. I've already started calling her Morse."

"And what was her response to that?" Lilly asked, tucking into the roast chicken the waitress had just served.

"She said, in case it had escaped my notice, she was female. So I've to try and find a suitable female equivalent or I run the risk of losing my inside woman at the station. The only one I could come up with was Miss Marple. But she wasn't an official detective, just a very clever and observant amateur sleuth. Rather like you, Lilly."

"Oh, please don't start, Archie. I'm trying to forget all about it after what happened the last time."

"Ah, yes," he said, becoming serious. "I heard all about that, Lilly. I'm sorry. Are things better between you and your friends now?"

Lilly shrugged. "A bit. We're on reasonably good speaking terms at least. It will take them a long time to come to terms with it all, obviously. Sadly, I don't think our friendship will ever be what it was."

"I'm sure they will come round, Lilly. It will just take time, like you say. So, how are the wedding plans coming along?"

"How do you know about that?"

She was surprised Archie knew about the wedding, considering they'd hardly spoken during the last month. Admittedly Plumpton Mallet was a small town, but Archie wasn't interested in the general goings on, especially if there wasn't a crime involved that he could get his teeth into, investigate and report.

"I have been invited," he said.

"Have you? Oh, that's great, Archie. On the bride or the groom's side?"

"Groom. I know Edmund of old, although not especially well. A long time ago, when dinosaurs still roamed the earth," Lilly laughed, Archie was barely five years older than she was. "Before I became a crime reporter, I did a piece on a mid-level housing development that was to be built in the next town. It was corrupt to the core, with planners, officials and builders all taking a cut. The proposal put forward listed high quality building products, but as is the wont of the greedy, I found out sub-standard materials were actually to be used in order to inflate their bottom line, which would make the buildings dangerous. A highly dubious practice, but sadly quite common. It got stopped in its tracks, thankfully. But Edmund was initially looking to invest. He saw my piece and rang me at the paper asking if I'd meet him for a drink. I did, and I told him all the real stuff that was going on behind the scenes. Things I couldn't put in my article otherwise we'd, the paper and probably me personally, would have been on the receiving end of a lawsuit. Naturally, he pulled out otherwise he'd have lost a pretty packet. He credits me with him not losing his shirt."

"Well done, Archie. I don't remember that. Have you met is fiancé Yasemin? It's her I'm working with."

"I have. They make a lovely couple. They seem very happy together. Edmund was smitten, as I recall."

Lilly was pleased to hear the groom was as much in love with his bride as she was with him. After witnessing so much horror over the previous few months, it was wonderful to be able to focus on something joyful.

"I'm a little concerned to hear his uncle is attending, though," Archie said, taking the last bite of his dinner and dabbing his mouth with the napkin.

"His uncle? Why, Archie?" Lilly said, a knot growing in her stomach. Poor Yasemin already had to contend with her mother not coming and Edmund's cousin letting her down. She definitely didn't need another difficult relative to deal with.

"Uncle Christopher. He and Edmund had a huge falling out a couple of years ago. Edmund sent him an invitation to his wedding out of a sense of duty, I think, never expecting him to confirm. But there's quite a bit of drama within Edmund Rogers' family."

"Do you know what happened between them?"

"No idea. But Edmund's a bit jittery about him attending. It's my understanding they've not spoken since."

"It's Yasemin I feel sorry for. She's having to plan most of this on her own. You know one of Edmund's cousins has let her down badly at the last minute? I can't remember her name now, but she was quite nasty on the phone when we were shopping for decor recently."

Archie snorted. "I bet I can guess who that was. Rachel Miles, by any chance?"

"Yes, Rachel, that's it. How did you know?"

"She's a brat of the first order. I don't know what her problem is, but she doesn't seem to like Yasemin very much."

"I can't understand why," Lilly said. "She really is lovely. Do you think it's because she's been married before?"

"Who knows? But I've met Mirac, and I think he's is genuinely fond of both Yasemin and Edmund. I just hope

24

the others can see how well suited they are on the day. Now, enough shop talk for you, you're here to relax and forget all about work. They do an excellent chocolate mousse here, Miss Tweed. And I shan't take no for an answer."

Lilly knew it was pointless to argue, so allowed the waitress to bring her the dessert. One mouthful and she was in heaven. It was every bit as good as Archie had promised.

She stayed for a further hour, putting the world to rights with her friend over a cappuccino, then bid him farewell. The following night was to be a rehearsal dinner of sorts to allow Yasemin to get to know her future in-laws a bit better in a less formal atmosphere prior to the wedding. She'd been hired to cater for that as well and wanted to make sure she was well rested. The weekend ahead was going to be a hectic one.

Chapter Four

THE REHEARSAL DINNER was taking place at the same venue where the wedding was to be held. A large family estate on the other side of the river belonging to a relative of Edmund's. It was built in the late 1700s and sat in two hundred acres of parkland, with two working farms and two lakes included. Set on a hillside with a large expanse of woodland to its rear, the views from the front showed tantalising glimpses of Plumpton Mallet town nestled in the valley below, and the expanse of moorland on the horizon opposite.

Lilly, Stacey and Bethany arrived early to set up and were greeted by the owner, a young man named Bruce. He looked slightly frazzled to Lilly when he opened the door to welcome them, and she wondered if he'd bitten off more than he could chew by offering his home for the wedding ceremony.

"You must be Lilly Tweed?" he said, offering his hand, before also shaking hands with Bethany and Stacey, then inviting them all inside.

"You have a very beautiful home," Lilly said. "I expect Edmund and Yasemin are thrilled to be able to have their wedding here, aren't they?"

Bruce nodded. "They are. Yasemin in particular loves the place. I only inherited it last year, not long after they got engaged. It belonged to my mother's side of the family. I'm still getting used to taking care of such a large concern."

"From what I can see, you're doing an excellent job." Bethany said. "Perhaps you could show us where to set up?"

Bruce nodded. "Of course. If you'd like to follow me. They've chosen the breakfast room for the rehearsal dinner. The Ceremony will take place in the courtyard and then on to the ballroom for the reception lunch and the evening buffet and party afterwards."

Stacey glanced at Lilly with a huge grin and raised eyebrows.

The breakfast room was larger than the entirety of Lilly's cottage and Stacey's flat combined, and the young American girl's eyes were on stalks as they entered. At the far end was a large, stone, inglenook fireplace with a flower and vine motif chiselled expertly into the chimney breast.

Several small, arched mullion windows, which wouldn't have looked out of place in a country church, were set into the two external walls, and looked out over the majestic countryside. The old, uneven walls were painted a clotted cream colour, giving the room a warm and cosy feel despite its size and the fifteen tables scattered around waiting to be laid. And to top it off, a large central chandelier with sparkling crystals hung from the double height ceiling. Matching wall sconces appeared every several feet. It was absolutely beautiful and perfect for the occasion.

"Wow!" Stacey said, hands on hips as she gazed in awe around the room. "You Brits sure know how to live. I'd love a place like this."

Bruce laughed. "Don't wish it on yourself. You'd be surprised how much money it takes to keep a place like this running. Believe me, it's more of a millstone at the moment. Edmund and Yasemin's wedding is a bit of an experiment actually, to see if I can do paid events in the future to help with the upkeep."

"Sounds like a plan," Stacey said, nodding. "So, it's been in your family for ever?"

"No, it actually belonged to some very distant relative I don't remember on my mother's side. My parents were the ones who inherited, but having just retired and intending to travel, they didn't want to be saddled with it. So, they offered it to me. I accepted, although I admit I was very naïve regarding what I was getting into."

"I think your idea for private functions and corporate events is a good one. You could even open up the grounds for picnics. There are plenty of stately homes that are successful doing that sort of thing," Lilly said.

Bruce nodded. "That's the long-term plan. Anyway, I'll let you get on. I'll be in my office if you need anything further. The kitchen is along the hall from the foyer where you entered, toward the back of the house, then down the servants' stairs. It's fully equipped, so you should have everything you need."

The ladies thanked him and began to set up. Stacey and Bethany dealt with the floral arrangements, then Lilly sent them off to the kitchen to begin the food preparations, while she set the tables. This was a much smaller affair than the wedding dinner, but no less important. It was almost like a practice run for the big event and Lilly was determined everything would be perfect.

$\mathcal{S}$HE WAS JUST folding the last of the deep burgundy damask napkins into a rose shape, which she placed in a gold and white teacup, when Yasemin entered.

"Oh, Lilly, it's all just beautiful," she said. "Exactly what I imagined."

The bride had chosen a distinctly exotic feel for the rehearsal dinner, the actual wedding meal being a typically English affair, with crisp white tablecloths and napkins, cut crystal glassware and tea rose floral arrangements. But tonight, in deliberate contrast, the tables were dressed in deep blue satin cloths with burgundy and gold table runners. The tea and signature cocktails were to be served in the tea cups, but there was an array of cranberry glasses with gilt rims for water, wine, and other beverages. Tall candelabras with dark red and blue candles finished the tables off.

"Yasemin, you look simply amazing," Lilly replied. Taking in the stunning floor length white and burgundy velvet bindalli dress. It was covered in incredibly ornate gold embroidery and hand sewn with hundreds of gold and silver beads. Finished with a gold belt as intricately detailed as the rest of the ensemble and a square shape of cloth placed on her head.

"Thank you so much," Yasemin said, a little embarrassed. "I had planned to wear a typically English tea dress, but I did a video call with my mother and the rest of the family and it seemed appropriate to give a nod to my cultural heritage. It helped appease her, I think. Although she wasn't happy I chose to forgo the traditional henna."

"I'm sorry. Is your mother still giving you a difficult time?"

Yasemin shrugged. "It is her loss, Lilly. Edmund is a wonderful man and we are perfectly matched if only my mother could see it. Edmund," she called out, turning to greet the young man who'd just entered the room. "Come and meet Lilly."

Lilly did vaguely recognise Edmund as she thought she'd might. He'd been to The Tea Emporium a couple of times since she'd opened while in town visiting his cousin.

"I think we've met, haven't we?" he said, slightly uncertain as he held out his hand to shake hers.

"We have, though a while ago. Peppermint and Rooibos teas, if I remember rightly?"

"Yes, that's right. Goodness, you've got a good memory. I must also thank you for looking after my wife-to-be so well recently," he added, pulling Yasemin in for a hug and kissing the top of her head.

Lilly smiled. "You're both very welcome. Now, everything is ready in here, and Bethany and Stacey are already in the kitchen preparing the dinner. I'll go and join them. I have cocktails and teas to make."

"Everyone should be here soon," Yasemin said excitedly. "Thank you, Lilly. Let us know if you need anything."

"I will."

In the kitchen she informed the others the main couple had arrived and the rest of the guests were due imminently. "And they love the decor in the breakfast room. I didn't realise Yasemin had chosen the colour scheme to compliment her bindalli. She must have known she'd relent when she spoke to her mother. She looks stunning."

"It's great when it all comes together," Stacey said, chopping four different types of tomatoes for Bethany. The soup course was to be tomato and basil with a secret ingredient Bethany wouldn't share, no matter how many times Lilly and Stacey asked.

Lilly started on the cocktails and happened to glance over at Bethany just as she rolled up her sleeves. She had an interesting tattoo on the inside of her left arm.

"Is that a wave?" she asked, reaching for a lemon.

"What?"

"On your arm."

Bethany smiled, holding up her arm. "It is. A stylised version, not everyone recognises it."

"I've been thinking about a tattoo," Stacey said. "What made you go for a wave?"

"My brother and me got matching ones when we were in our late teens. Some of our favourite childhood memories were spent at the beach."

"That's a nice story," Lilly said. "I didn't know you had a brother, Bethany."

"He passed away," she replied, gazing at the tattoo for a moment.

"I'm so sorry. I didn't realise."

"Don't worry, it was a long time ago. Right, another ten minutes and I think we'll be ready. Let's get this show on the road with the drinks, shall we?"

*T*HE GUESTS MINGLED and chatted for half an hour or so, while Stacey and Lilly served special cocktails and teas. As everyone began to take their seats, they moved back to the kitchen to collect the soup Bethany was pouring into bowls.

"That looks and smells fantastic," Lilly said. "I hope there's some left for us later."

"Don't worry, I made extra."

With trays loaded, Bethany placed them in the dumb waiter and pressed the up button.

"I am so relieved they've got one of these," Lilly said. "I didn't relish going up that flight of stairs with trays of scalding soup."

Upstairs, Lilly and Stacey retrieved the trays and carried them to the breakfast room, leaving Bethany in the kitchen to deal with the next course. They served the wedding couple first, then moved round the tables to the other guests. However, one of the chairs remained empty. The nameplate read *Christopher Rogers*.

"Oh, did Edmund's uncle not make it?" she asked the woman seated to the right of the space, placing a bowl in front of her.

"It looks that way, doesn't it?" she replied, a little sarcastically. "Although I didn't expect him to."

Lilly read the woman's place card. "Oh, you're Edmund's cousin, Rachel?"

She received a mildly annoyed look in response. "Do I look as though I'm related to the bride?"

Lilly smiled tightly. "No, but not everyone here is related, are they?"

The woman smirked, conceding the point. "That's true. Yes, I'm Edmund's cousin on his mother's side. You're the one who ended up sorting out the place settings, aren't you? Lilly something?"

"Yes. Lilly Tweed."

"Thank you." She replied, but said no more on the matter before turning to the soup. The conversation was obviously over.

As Lilly moved to serve the last guest, the door opened and a tall, burly man entered, dragging his feet. There were a few quick glances his way, but in the main, no one had noticed the late arrival. He took the empty place next to Rachel.

"The prodigal uncle returns," Rachel scoffed, and it seemed to Lilly that Rachel's default was sarcasm. "I didn't think you'd come."

"Don't start, Rachel. Of course I came."

Lilly placed a bowl of soup in front of him, and with all the guests now attended to, reconvened with Bethany and Stacey in the kitchen.

"Wow," Stacey breathed. "I can't believe the drama going on in there already."

"Are you talking about Mirac?" Lilly asked.

"He's just happy to see Yasemin marrying for love, isn't he? So he can find someone he wants to be married to, as well." Bethany said. "I think it's amazing he happily divorced her and introduced her to Edmund."

"I don't know about that," Stacey said. "I think it might have been the other way around. I caught him looking at her loads of times. I think he's still in love with her and regrets they split up. But that's not what I was talking about. I meant the uncle who came in late. It's obvious no one wants him here. I'm surprised he came."

"I don't think we should gossip about them. It's not very professional. Especially if we get caught," Lilly said.

But Bethany was already adding to the conversation.

"I found out from Bruce what really happened there," she said. And Stacey leaned in, eager to hear what she had to say. "Apparently, the reason he and Edmund haven't spoken for so long is because Christopher's mother wrote him out of the will and left everything to Edmund."

"Seriously?" Lilly said, interested despite her previous comment.

"There's more. Apparently Edmund's parents died when he was a child and he and his sister Ellie were brought up by their grandparents, Christopher's parents. Christopher had a big falling out with his father and when his father died, he didn't go to the funeral. His mother was furious, as you can imagine, and promptly wrote him out of the will."

"Wow, that must have been some falling out. But not going to your dad's funeral is really bad," Stacey said.

"So, Christopher is angry because Edmund and his sister are going to get his inheritance?" Lilly said.

Bethany nodded. "Basically. And, what's more important is that Christopher's mother died a couple of weeks ago. I think the only reason he's here is to try to talk Edmund out of the money."

"Well, I hope he has the decency not to spoil the wedding," Lilly said. "I didn't realise Edmund had a sister. Why isn't she here for the wedding?"

"I've no idea. That's all I found out."

"I should give my condolences to Edmund for the loss of his grandmother."

"I don't think that's a good idea, Lilly," Bethany said. "I found this out in secret, remember. We're not supposed to know. I don't want us to get a reputation for gossip. We'll not get any more work if we do."

"Yes, you're right. If he wanted us to know, he would have said something. I'll keep quiet."

"It's for the best. Now, the main course is done," Bethany said, bending and retrieving a vast array of meat and vegetable dishes from the ovens. These would be placed on the tables for the guests to help themselves. "Could you clear away the soup course and send the dishes down? I'll load up the main courses and send them up. That way you don't have to trail up and down the stairs."

"Great idea," Lilly said. "I don't think my knees will take much more trooping up and down those stairs."

With the main course served and the dishwasher running its first cycle, the three of them sat down to a meal of their own, soup and crusty bread. An hour later, the guests had finished and the three of them started to clear up the breakfast room while the wedding party made their way outside to the courtyard for the rehearsal.

❦

"I THINK THAT WENT very well. The food was excellent, Bethany." Lilly said. "I'm glad we had the chance to practice with something smaller before the bigger event. Are all your staff ready?"

"Of course. I've been training them. They're all looking forward to it."

Bruce Rogers entered, looking even more exhausted than he had when they'd arrived. "I just wanted to pop in and say thanks to you all for tonight. I know both Yasemin and Edmund were very happy with how it went. They would have come themselves, but they're preoccupied with the rehearsal at the moment. They'll speak to you before you leave, I'm sure."

"We're glad we could be part of it," Lilly replied, then turned when they heard shouting coming from outside.

She, along with Stacey and Bruce, and with Bethany bringing up the rear, dashed out to the gardens where they found a shocked Edmund, his head drenched in what appeared to be red wine.

"For crying out loud, Christopher," Mirac shouted, putting himself between his friend and his estranged uncle.

"He deserved it. I'll not put up with his insolence."

"All I said was we'd talk about it later. Not tonight, or at my wedding, you oaf!" Edmund shouted, wiping dripping wine from his face and chin.

"You're out of line, Christopher," Rachel said. "That was inappropriate, not to mention childish. Why would you attend Edmund's rehearsal dinner if you're going to treat him like this? Or was that part of your petty plan?"

"You're one to talk," Christopher retorted.

"That's enough! Go back to your hotel and calm down, or I'll drag you there myself."

"You and whose army? You little brat."

"Don't push me, Christopher, or you'll be sorry. You're not my uncle," Rachel hissed, fire in her eyes.

Christopher took a step back, stunned at the vehemence in Rachel's voice and the look of hatred on her face. "Fine," he said, looking at Edmund and jabbing a finger in his direction. "You and me, we'll talk, and soon. You and your sister are a couple of thieves and you won't get away with it."

"I didn't steal anything from you, Christopher, and you know it. If you'd wanted your parents' money, then perhaps you should have been there for them like I was. I don't know why I invited you. I should have known you'd behave like this."

"Watch your back, Edmund," Christopher said between clenched teeth, then spun on his heels and stalked away in the direction of his car.

Bruce made his way over to Edmund and laid a hand on his shoulder. "Are you all right?"

"I'm fine. Just covered in wine. My shirt and suit are ruined, but I suppose it could have been worse."

Yasemin hurried over to her fiancé. "I'm just glad he didn't hurt you, Edmund. I can't believe he did that. What a childish thing to do." She turned to Rachel. "Thank you for standing up to him, Rachel. It was brave considering the foul mood he was in."

Rachel sniffed, then turned away, plainly dismissing Yasemin in front of everyone.

Bruce cleared his throat in an attempt to salvage the situation. "Well, what's a wedding without a bit of family drama and spilled drink?" The assembled guests chuckled, the tension diffused. "I think it's time we let these two love birds go so they can get a good night's sleep before the big day. Thank you all for coming."

The crowd said their farewells to the couple and dispersed. Lilly and Stacey returned to the kitchen. It appeared Bethany had already gone before them, to finish the cleaning up and confirm the arrangements for the next day. Lilly fervently hoped Uncle Christopher would stay away from the actual wedding. He'd caused enough trouble already.

Chapter Five

*T*HE WEDDING DAY had finally arrived and very early in the morning Lilly was in the back storeroom of The Tea Emporium, packing the teas and china ready to be transported to the venue. Stacey appeared blurry eyed, hugging a large mug of coffee. Lilly laughed.

"Good morning, sleepyhead."

"It's still the middle of the night in my book."

"It's quarter to seven."

"Like I said. Still night," she said through a humongous yawn. "By the way, I stayed up last night and made a new sign for the shop door. It explains why we're closed today and promotes our new catering service."

"That looks excellent, Stacey. Well done. Now, finish your coffee and wake up a bit. We need to get this lot over to Bruce's house. How's Earl?"

"He's fine. Safe in the flat with everything he needs. I think he likes the idea of being able to sleep on my bed all day. Lucky him, that's what I say."

Stacey quickly drank her coffee and picked up the first of the boxes, taking it out the back door to Lilly's waiting car. Half an hour later, the car was packed and Lilly was getting ready to set off when Stacey dashed back inside. A moment later she hurried back, make-up bag in hand.

"I'll do it on the way over," she said.

Lilly couldn't help but laugh as Stacey tried to apply the cosmetics on the bumpy road.

"I'll wait," she said eventually, wiping lipstick off her cheek and mascara from her eyebrow.

Lilly drove across the bridge which spanned the river, then turned right. Twenty minutes later, she turned left up the steep hill and took another left into the entrance of the estate.

"Oh look, Bethany's already here. And I thought we were early," Stacey said, stifling another yawn.

Lilly parked next to the catering vehicle and the two of them began to unload the car. Lilly sent Stacey to the kitchen with the foodstuffs while she took the china and tablecloths to the ballroom. She was returning to her car for the final box when she saw a running figure out of the corner of her eye. She turned, expecting to see Stacey, but was shocked to see Yasemin charging from the house. She called out, but the girl was too far away to hear her. Lilly had a sinking feeling in the pit of her stomach and set off in pursuit, finally catching up with her in a grove of cherry trees.

"Yasemin, whatever is the matter?"

She was hunched over and in floods of tears, make-up running down her cheeks and hair in a mess having shaken loose from the pins and clips which had made the beautiful bridal 'up-do.'

"I don't want to talk about it. I just want to get as far away from here as possible."

"Surely it can't be that bad," Lilly said, guiding her to a nearby bench. It was secluded so they could avoid the prying eyes of staff and delivery personnel. She glanced at her watch and saw there was still plenty of time before the ceremony was due to begin. She needed to get whatever this was sorted out, and soon, if there was to be a wedding at all.

"Now, tell me what's happened, Yasemin. Perhaps I can help?"

The girl wiped her eyes and sniffed. Lilly handed her a handkerchief, and she noisily blew her nose before beginning to speak in breathy, raspy tones.

"I thought we were happy. I was ready to commit my whole life to him, Lilly. We weren't supposed to have secrets from one another."

Yasemin stopped talking, taking deep, shuddering breaths, fighting more tears. Lilly took her hand.

"I assume you are talking about Edmund?"

Yasemin nodded. "I found something this morning."

"Go on. I promise it won't go any further, but I can't help if I don't know what's wrong."

"Edmund was looking for the cuff-links his grandfather had given him. He wanted to wear them today but couldn't find them. I thought they might be in his study so went to look this morning. Oh Lilly, I found some invoices, lots and lots of them. Edmund is in serious debt and owes thousands and thousands of pounds. I can't believe he didn't tell me. I can't marry a man who would lie to me. How can I begin my married life knowing we owe so much money? It will take years to pay it off. What if he is just marrying me for my money? I don't have enough to pay off the whole debt, but my family does. Does he expect me to ask them? I came here and was getting ready when I realised I just couldn't go through with it. I cannot marry Edmund, Lilly. The truth is the most important thing in a relationship and he deliberately kept this from me."

"Oh, Yasemin," Lilly said. "First of all, I can tell you that Edmund loves you to distraction. It's immediately apparent to anyone who meets you both. Secondly, and please don't take this the wrong way, I think you're jumping to conclusions without knowing the full facts. Perhaps he's in negotiations with the company because the work they've invoiced for wasn't up to scratch? Or they are old invoices and the recent ones he has paid but filed somewhere else. You won't know the truth until you've spoken to him about them. I really do think you need to sit down and talk to him about it, give him the benefit of the doubt and the chance to tell you his side of the story. It could be something as simple as not wanting to worry you."

Yasemin sniffed, but had calmed down enough for Lilly to know she had been listening and was thinking seriously about what she'd suggested. Seconds later, they heard hurried footsteps approaching. It was Edmund. When he saw Yasemin had been crying, his face fell and he rushed to her side.

"Yasemin, what's wrong? I've been looking for you everywhere. Someone said they'd seen you rushing out here in tears. What has happened?"

Lilly moved away to give the couple some space to talk, but stayed near at hand in case she was needed.

"How could you keep something so important from me, Edmund?"

Edmund shook his head. "I don't know what you mean. What have I done?"

"I found the invoices when I was looking for your cuff-links. You owe thousands of pounds, Edmund. How could you keep this debt from me?"

"Oh, Yasemin. I was going to tell you, I just wanted to wait until we were married first, that's all."

"Why? So I could pay them off? My family may be wealthy but I cannot and will not ask them to repay your debt."

"I would never expect nor ask you to. Surely you know me better than that?"

Yasemin sniffed. "I thought I did."

Edmund took her hand. "Let me explain, darling. I actually do have the money to pay the invoices, but it will leave my company almost insolvent if I do that. There were escalating costs, which were the builder's fault, but part of the blame is mine because I didn't negotiate a flat fee. However, I am working with them and we've agreed to a payment in a few weeks time. I'll have my inheritance by then and we'll still have more money than we can spend, even after I've paid my debts. I promise you, you're not marrying a debtor. I would never ask you to take on debts I owe. I love you, Yasemin, and want to spend the rest of my life with you. Everything is going to be fine."

"Do you promise?"

"I promise," Edmund said. Giving her a hug. "Now, let's get back to the house. I can't wait to see you walk down the aisle and finally become my wife."

They rose together and sauntered back to the house, hand in hand. Lilly breathed a sigh of relief. Crisis averted. She set off back to the house at a jog. The time spent with Yasemin had delayed her. She just had to hope she could get everything done in time for the reception.

*L*ILLY DASHED INTO the ballroom and came to a skidding halt, shocked to see most of the work had already been done. The brilliant white Irish linen cloths covered the tables. The majority of the place settings were laid as well as the central floral arrangements, which had arrived that morning as the florist had promised. Five crystal glasses were placed at each setting, for water, champagne, red, white and dessert wine. Arranged in a slight curve to prevent the layout from looking dull and to save on space. The silverware had been polished and their layout almost completed, and the lovers' table at the top of the room looked stunning. Every bit as perfect as Lilly had imagined.

Stacey appeared with the last set of china and glasses. "Lilly, where have you been? This was not easy to set up. You better check I did it right. I get lost after the fish fork."

Lilly laughed. "Stacey, you are an absolute gem. Thank you. I'm sorry you had to deal with it all yourself. Yasemin got a case of the wobbles, but it's all fine now. And this is almost perfect, well done."

She swapped out two of the knives and their complementary forks, and adjusted a napkin folded into a swan, then declared it perfect. Stacey went round the tables and adjusted the other settings while Lilly laid the last one. When that was complete, Lilly added the trinkets Yasemin had bought to the lover's table and it was all finished.

Back in the kitchen, the place was a flurry of activity with caterers preparing the food. Lilly found Bethany in the middle, directing the proceedings.

"Where were you?" she asked Lilly when she saw her. "Stacey was looking for you."

"It's okay, she found me. I was having a private conversation with Yasemin. A slight case of cold feet, but it's all fine now."

"What do you mean, cold feet? She's not called it off, has she?"

"No, nothing like that. Don't panic. Just a few pre-wedding jitters, that's all," Lilly replied, remembering her promise to Yasemin to keep it a secret. "Everything's running to schedule."

Bethany nodded and went back to organising the food with military precision. With Stacey and Lilly having done as much as they could for the time being, they moved to the courtyard to watch the ceremony. Stacey went to talk to one of the waitresses, a fellow student, who was taking a break to watch the service from a secluded spot, and a moment later Lilly was joined by Archie.

"Doesn't this look fabulous?" he said, waving an arm at the tented pergola strung with fairy lights and twining vines with silk roses woven through them. The chairs were covered in pale pink silk with large bows at the back, and the aisle was scattered with rose petals. Ushers, dressed in smart grey suits with silk waistcoats, were showing guests to their seats. At the front, a small dais waited for the bride and groom, with a large waterfall display of roses, white lilies and assorted greenery at the back underneath an arbour. It looked and smelled heavenly.

"It's gorgeous, Archie," Lilly replied. "And I must say you scrub up extremely well, my friend. You look very dapper."

Archie was dressed in a charcoal grey pinstripe suit with a cream waistcoat, navy blue silk formal ascot and matching pocket square.

"Thank you, my dear. It's nice to have an excuse to get out and dust off the formal attire once in a while. You, however, look a bit flustered, if you don't mind me saying so. Is everything running like a well-oiled machine behind the scenes or is it all chaos and anarchy?"

"It's all fine. I just had a few last minute tasks to do. You know, setting tables, mixing cocktails, stopping the bride from fleeing," she answered with a grin.

"Wait, what? The bride was going to run away? Tell me more," Archie said, sidling in closer with exaggerated aplomb and making Lilly laugh. She filled him in on Yasemin's concerns, but omitted the part about the finances.

"So, Lilly Tweed saves the day!"

"Hush, Archie, not too loud. I don't want Edmund's cousins hearing about Yasemin's cold feet."

Archie mimed locking his lips and throwing the key over his shoulder and Lilly giggled. A woman turned and glowered at her.

"I'm terribly sorry," Archie said. "I'll try to keep her quiet, but she doesn't get out much I'm afraid, and she's over excited."

The woman turned back to face the front and Lilly playfully punched Archie on the arm. "I will get my own back for that, Archie Brown," she whispered quietly, just as the string quartet struck up the wedding march.

"Better get back to my seat," Archie said. "I'll catch you later."

He had just managed to sit when Esen, Yasemin's maid of honour, began her approach down the aisle, dressed in a vintage style ankle length tea dress in pale cream with yellow roses and deep green leaves, carrying the bouquet Lilly had designed with the florist.

As the bride followed, alone as her parents weren't in attendance, everyone stood and smiled, some taking photos with their phones, while the professional photographer Edmund had hired for the day darted about getting images of the bride and the guests. There was also a videographer doing the same on the opposite side. Edmund certainly wasn't taking any chances. Nothing would be missed and everything recorded for posterity.

The wedding gown was a stunning champagne coloured vintage design, with a tight, detailed bodice and full skirt, which accentuated her small waist. Made from Peau De Soie taffeta and organza, trimmed with Duchess satin and encrusted with pearls and diamante. The organza sleeves were full length, with a long tight cuff, fastened with five pearl buttons. Her shoes were of ivory satin, embellished with pearls. It was the most exquisite dress Lilly had ever seen. And judging by the audible intake of breath from the front, Edmund thought so too.

The ceremony went perfectly, with no one objecting, and Lilly let out a breath she hadn't realised she'd been holding.

After the couple's kiss and their return walk down the aisle where they were showered with rose petal confetti, Archie came back to stand with Lilly.

"That went rather well," he said. "And that gown. It reminds me of the recent marriage of our royal princess."

Lilly nodded. "I think that's where they idea came from. Gosh, I can't tell you how relieved I am that that went well, Archie. Especially considering what happened at the rehearsal."

"Oh? What happened?"

"Uncle Christopher threw a glass of red wine over Edmund, ruining his shirt and suit. He was told in no uncertain terms to leave."

"Oh dear. Well, I can't say I'm surprised. What about dear cousin Rachel? She added fuel to the fire, I suppose?"

"No, actually. She practically threatened Christopher with a good hiding if he didn't calm down and would have dragged him away herself if he hadn't seen sense and left of his own accord. She was most definitely on Edmund's side."

"Well, that does surprise me."

"She ruined it though by snubbing Yasemin very obviously in front of everyone when Yasemin thanked her for her help."

"And there's the Rachel we all know and love," Archie said sarcastically, shaking his head. "Let's hope that's the end of the drama. It's about time I enjoyed a good knees up courtesy of someone else's wallet for a change."

Chapter Six

THE FOOD IN the evening would be a help your-self style buffet available for an hour between seven thirty and eight thirty, catering as it would to additional friends and distant relatives. But the formal sit down dinner for the main wedding guests was really a lunch time affair. Drinks orders were being placed with the waiting staff and Lilly was happily mixing the signature cocktails and teas behind a makeshift bar, alongside two other barmen who had been hired by Bethany.

The meal was hard work for the staff, but in the end it was deemed to be a resounding success by everyone. A few hours later everyone dispersed to rest, freshen up or change outfits before the evening party, and Lilly, Stacey, Bethany and the rest of the staff made short work of clearing everything away and setting up the ballroom for the evening, before having their own lunch and well-earned break.

At seven o'clock Lilly was once again behind the bar, this time with Stacey at her side, as the first of the evening reception guests began to arrive, and by nine, after everyone had availed themselves of the food and the catering staff were starting the clear up, the ballroom was in full swing, with the live band, having played a slow number for the bride and groom's first dance, now belting out tunes from the thirties and forties.

"They look so happy together, Lilly. I'm so glad you were able to talk Yasemin round earlier. It could have been a disaster."

"I can't take the credit, Stacey. That was all Edmund. But look at her face. She is blissfully happy. I think she would have regretted it forever if she'd run away."

"Can I have a pink gin fizz, darling?" an elderly man, ironically dressed like a Prohibition era gangster, asked her. Even more apt considering she also happened to be serving alcohol in teacups.

"Of course," she replied with a smile, reaching for the cocktail shaker.

Just at that minute, the ballroom was plunged into darkness. After a few faltering notes, the band stopped playing altogether and Bruce made an announcement. "Apologies everyone. If you all remain where you are for a moment, I'll go and see what the problem is. Don't worry, I'll have the lights back on in no time."

"I bet a power cut wasn't in Bethany's meticulous plans," Lilly said to Stacey. "She'll go mad when she gets back to the kitchen as everything works on electricity."

"Hopefully Bruce will get the power back on soon."

A few minutes ticked by and just when Lilly thought the party would have to end, the lights came back on. A split second later, there was a ghastly scream.

"That was Yasemin," Lilly said, dashing from behind the bar.

She stopped in shock at the scene before her; Yasemin kneeling in the centre of the ballroom next to the prostrate figure of Edmund lying in a pool of blood with a knife at his side.

"Oh, please, no," Lilly gasped.

The next seconds were a state of panic as reality dawned on the crowd. Archie Brown shouted for everyone to stand back while he telephoned the police.

"He's dead!" Yasemin screamed, staring in horror at her bloodied hands.

Lilly dashed over to her, "Yasemin, get up. Come on, there's nothing you can do for him now."

She pulled the frightened girl from the floor and practically carried her to the nearest powder room, where she put her in a chair and began to soak hand towels in the sink to clean her up.

Yasemin was practically catatonic as she wiped her hands, the smudges on her face, and made the best attempt she could to get the blood off the front of her wedding gown. Stacey arrived ten minutes later.

"Lilly, the ambulance and several police officers have arrived. Bonnie's in charge," she said softly.

"I don't understand what happened," Yasemin said, speaking for the first time since Lilly had taken her from the scene. "We were dancing, then the lights went out and I couldn't find him. Is he really dead? No, he can't be. Please tell me he's all right?"

Stacey shook her head. "I don't know. The paramedics are with him now."

She lurched up. "I need to go to him. He'll need me."

She staggered forward a couple of steps, but her knees buckled. Stacey and Lilly caught her, waited a moment while she felt steadier, then, when she wouldn't take no for an answer, helped her back out to the ballroom. Lilly saw Edmund's body had already been covered with a sheet and a stretcher was on standby. They guided Yasemin to the nearest chair and were immediately joined by Bonnie.

"Is he dead?" Yasemin asked the detective.

Bonnie nodded and crouched down to be at eye level with the stricken bride. "Yes. I'm sorry. It was very quick. He was already gone by the time the paramedics arrived."

Yasemin covered her face and began to weep.

"What happened?" Stacey asked. "One minute they're dancing, the lights go off and when they come back on he's..."

Bonnie stood up. "He's been stabbed in the neck," she replied quietly. "Yasemin, you were with him. Did you see anything?"

"No, nothing. He stepped away from me and I couldn't find him in the dark. I nearly tripped over him just before the lights came back on."

She dissolved into tears once more and Mirac, obviously unable to stay away any longer, came charging over. He enveloped Yasemin in a strong embrace, and Lilly saw her slump into him, grateful for the contact, while she sobbed uncontrollably on his shoulder.

"Did you two see anything?" Bonnie asked Lilly and Stacey.

"I didn't," Lilly said, looking at Stacey, who also shook her head. "We were both busy serving behind the bar. We had no idea anything was wrong until the lights came back on and Yasemin screamed. The guests seated at the tables near to where they were dancing might have noticed something, though."

"You!" Yasemin suddenly shouted. Wrenching herself away from Mirac and pointing an accusatory finger at a man in the crowd. As one, Lilly, Stacey and Bonnie turned and came face to face with Edmund's Uncle Christopher.

"**I** NEVER TOUCHED HIM, Yasemin. I know you're upset, but I don't appreciate you accusing me of murder!"

"I don't believe you," Yasemin countered. "You're the one after his inheritance. It's the only reason you came to our wedding. Admit it! We only invited you out of a sense of obligation, but after the way you behaved at the rehearsal, we should have made sure you couldn't attend today. You did this. You took Edmund from me."

"All right, calm down," Bonnie said, putting herself between the two. "Yasemin," she said gently. "Unless you have definitive proof of what you're accusing this man of, I advise you to keep quiet. Now, go and get changed. I suggest we discuss this further at the station. And you," she said, turning to Christopher. "You can come too. The rest of you, please stay where you are. My officers and I will be coming to you all shortly to take your details and your statements. After that, you will be allowed to leave. However, I suggest you remain in town for the foreseeable future where you can be reached if we have further questions. That goes for staff as well as guests."

There was a collective groan from all those assembled, which Bonnie studiously ignored, although none of them dared complain out loud.

Lilly guided Yasemin away, offering to help her change and then drive her to the station.

In her room, while Lilly helped her out of her intricate dress, Yasemin vacillated between anger, disbelief, and tears.

"It must have been Christopher who killed Edmund. Who else would want him dead?"

Lilly kept quiet. She had no idea who was responsible, but Yasemin needed to vent. Eventually, she would tire herself out and perhaps begin to see things more clearly.

"Why don't you go and have a quick shower, Yasemin? I'll find something for you to wear, then we can go to the police station. All right?"

Yasemin nodded. At the same time there was a knock at the door and Esen entered, still wearing her tea dress.

"Yasemin, I came as soon as I could," she said, hugging her friend.

Yasemin began to cry again. Esen looked at Lilly.

"They are still asking questions of everyone downstairs. Edmund's uncle has been taken to the police station, but the lady detective is looking for you, I think."

"I'll go and talk to her. I'll let her know Yasemin won't be long. Can you help her get ready quickly?"

Esen nodded. "I can take her to the police station, too."

"Thank you." Lilly left and returned to the ground floor where she found those remaining guests the police still needed to speak to milling about in the hall. The ballroom had been closed off and designated as a crime scene for the time being. Bonnie saw her and approached.

"Yasemin is getting ready and will be down shortly. Esen, her maid of honour, is with her," Lilly said.

"Okay, thanks. We're almost done here. Christopher Rogers is already at the station. I had one of my officers take him. I'll be going shortly to speak with him. The body has been taken to the mortuary and I expect the pathologist will start the post-mortem tomorrow. Hopefully that will give us some answers, because apart from the blood on the floor, there's nothing in the ballroom that's helping."

"Are we able to carry on clearing everything away, then?"

Bonnie thought for a while, then nodded. "I'll have one of my officers accompany you to ensure everything is done by the book, but I don't see why not. However, I only want you, Stacey, and Bethany in there. No one else."

"Of course. I'll let them know."

As she left Bonnie, she spied Mirac leaning against a wall alone and looking badly shaken. She wandered over and asked if he was all right?

"No, of course I'm not. My good friend has been murdered. On his wedding day and right in front of me. That means I most likely know who did it. Have you any idea what that feels like?"

It was on the tip of Lilly's tongue to say, yes, she did, actually, but she thought better of it.

"But never mind me," Mirac continued with an impatient wave of his hand. "How is Yasemin?"

"Distraught. Esen is with her. She's taking her to the police station shortly."

"Esen can't be trusted to drive anyone anywhere. She's always getting lost at home, never mind somewhere she's never been before. I will drive Yasemin to the station."

He stalked off and took the stairs to the upper floor two at a time.

"Where is he going?" Bonnie asked, coming to stand with her.

"To get Yasemin. He'll drive her to the station. He thinks Esen will get lost if she tries it."

"I don't care how she gets there, as long as it's soon. I'm leaving now, Lilly, but if you find anything or remember something that will help, let me know immediately, will you?"

"Of course I will, Bonnie. I always do. Where did Archie get to, by the way? I've not seen him for a while."

"He left when the ambulance did. No doubt hunched over his typewriter as we speak, putting together an article for the next edition."

"He'll be careful, Bonnie, don't worry."

"I know he will. But I'm going to have to put a stop to any and all reporting for the time being."

"Oh dear. He will be disappointed."

"For now. But he'll cheer up when I promise him the exclusive."

Once Bonnie and the rest of the guests had finally left, Lilly made her way downstairs to the kitchen, where she found Bethany and Stacey drinking tea at the table, and a couple of Bethany's remaining staff leaning against the counter talking in hushed tones.

"What's happening?" Stacey asked.

Lilly explained the three of them could now finish clearing the ballroom under the supervision of one of Bonnie's officers, so they trooped back upstairs to begin the task. The others would remain in the kitchen to wash what they sent down via the dumb waiter. Any remaining untouched food would be packed up and returned to the cafe.

With just the three of them, the clearing of tables and cleaning up took a long time and it was after two o'clock in the morning before the last of the items was safely packed in the back of Lilly's car.

Having said goodbye to Bethany and dropped Stacey off at her flat, Lilly crawled into bed at just after three in the morning, exhausted. Her dreams filled with Edmund and his angry relatives.

Chapter Seven

*L*ILLY OBVIOUSLY COULDN'T know what the aftermath of the murder would be, but when she visited Bethany at her cafe a couple of days later, she wasn't expecting to discover they hadn't been paid in full for their services.

"I thought Edmund was giving you the final cheque before the ceremony?" Lilly said to Bethany.

"What? No, I thought you'd agreed to pick it up from Yasemin?"

Lilly had left Stacey running the shop while she ran errands. One of which was to pick up her share of the money from the final payment. She'd been intending to give Stacey a bonus for all the work she'd put in. It would help with the new books she would need when her autumn college term started. If it hadn't been for her, Lilly knew she wouldn't have been able to accept the job in the first place. Now it was obvious there had been a miscommunication between her and Bethany somewhere down the line. An error that could prove to be an extremely expensive mistake if it wasn't rectified soon.

"This is really awkward," Bethany said. "After what happened at the wedding, the last thing I want to do is ask Yasemin for the money."

"You and me both," Lilly said. "I can't imagine what the poor girl must be going through. It must be absolutely dreadful. But, and I know this sounds heartless, although I don't mean it to, it's a huge amount of money we are owed, Bethany. And neither of us can afford to lose it. We did an excellent job and need to be compensated accordingly. I'm afraid one of us is going to have to bite the bullet and ask for it."

"I hate to say it, Lilly, but you know Yasemin the best. You've become quite good friends with her over the course of planning the wedding. I really do think it would be better coming from you."

Lilly frowned. "I understand what you're saying, Bethany, but it could have the opposite effect. She might think our friendship means she can delay payment and I won't take offence."

"Well, we've got to do something. What about Stacey? Would she do it?"

"Of course not. I would never ask Stacey to do something I wasn't prepared to do myself. Besides, although I consider her a friend, she is also my employee. It's not her job to go cash chasing, it's mine."

"So you'll do it?"

Lilly sighed. She'd fallen right into that trap. "I'm not sure how yet, but yes, I suppose you can leave it with me."

"Thank you, Lilly. I really do appreciate it. Let me get you a coffee."

While Bethany went to make them both a cappuccino, Lilly wondered how she was going to get the money they were owed. Then her thoughts briefly turned to Bonnie and hoped she was nearer to finding out who was responsible. She was still mulling over the best way to approach Yasemin when Bethany returned with her drink and a slice of homemade cherry Bakewell.

"So were Edmund and Yasemin paying for everything, or was there some family help?" Bethany asked.

"They were doing it all themselves. Her family refused to help because it was a second wedding. As far as they were concerned, Mirac was the perfect son-in-law and they should never have split up. Edmund's family felt the contribution of the estate from Bruce was enough, I suppose."

"From what I understand," Bethany said. "Edmund's family didn't like the idea of him marrying Yasemin any more than her family liked the idea of her marrying him."

"Really?" Lilly said. "Why? Because she's a divorcee?"

"Actually, I got the impression his uncle and cousins didn't like the idea of him marrying someone who wasn't English."

Lilly was appalled. "You mean they're prejudiced? That's despicable."

But as Lilly thought more about Bethany's revelation, she found her surprise waning. She'd seen herself how some of Edmund's family had treated Yasemin. Particularly his cousin Rachel. She'd deliberately and conspicuously snubbed

Yasemin in public and been rude on at least one other occasion she'd witnessed. It was bad enough when she'd thought they didn't want him to marry a divorcee, but the real reason was far worse. Incomprehensible to Lilly. So, his family appeared to be loyal to him, but not to his chosen bride? She really hoped Yasemin wouldn't have to deal with them too much over the coming days. At least she had Mirac to lean on. It might be a little awkward, but he would be a staunch, much needed support in the near future. And by the sounds of it, she really could do with someone on her side.

"I need to get back to work, Lilly," Bethany said, interrupting her thoughts. "Let me know how it goes with Yasemin, won't you?"

Lilly nodded. "Yes, of course. Thanks for the coffee and cake."

Lilly left the cafe and mounted her bike. She had other errands to run. One of which was a stop at a local bakery.

*B*EFORE LEAVING HOME that morning, Lilly had loaded her bicycle with vegetables picked from her garden. One of the joys of working in a small town like Plumpton Mallet was the friendships cultivated with fellow business owners.

'The Loafer' was one such shop. Susanna, the bakery owner, had started giving Lilly speciality bread and stocking her teas in exchange for fresh carrots and other vegetables as she grew them. She used the carrots for one of her bestselling items, a fabulous carrot cake which usually sold out within an hour of the shop opening. Lilly's mouth watered at the thought of it.

Leaning her bike against the bakery window, she hefted the large bag of produce and went inside. As with The Tea Emporium, The Loafer was also double fronted with the door in the centre of two bay windows, but that's where the similarities ended. Whereas Lilly had chosen a vintage English design, Susanna had opted for a venetian style. The floor was a black and white chequered tile, and the walls to the left and right had murals of old venetian side streets and cafes. When you entered, you were greeted by a full length dark wood counter with glass display cabinets on top featuring mouth watering cakes and pastries.

Huge wicker baskets, hung at an angle across the back wall behind the counter, were filled with freshly baked loaves, cobs and baps of every imaginable flavour, both sweet and savory and dusted with fine flour or seeds. Above, a chalkboard was hanging with the regular price list, daily specials and a quote of the day, 'Bake the world a better place,' was the one for today. Sitting in each of the bay windows were two small wrought-iron tables with mosaic tiled tops, accompanied by two chairs to each.

At the sound of the door bell Susanna looked up and waved. There were a handful of customers inside, some queuing at the counter, others seated at the tables enjoying a coffee. Once she'd finished serving, Susanna lifted the counter top at the far end and came to greet Lilly.

"You've brought carrots, Lilly, and just in time, I've just finished the last lot. Thanks so much."

"You're very welcome."

"Now, what would you like in exchange? I've got a sun-dried tomato and Feta loaf, which is proving very popular. A Greek olive bread, or a new recipe four-cheese cob."

"They all sound wonderful, Susanna. I'll take whatever you suggest. I couldn't possibly choose between them."

Susanna smiled. "One of each, then. Have a seat while I take the carrots to the kitchen and make you up a bag."

Lilly took a seat at the only empty table while she waited. The Loafer had recently invested in a new addition, a coffee bar, which hadn't been present the last time Lilly had been in and the aroma of freshly ground coffee, mixed with the scent of baking, was making her stomach rumble. She waited while a young couple had been served, then wandered over.

"I'll have a large mochaccino to take out, please," she told the girl behind the counter. She was young, probably not much older than sixteen. No doubt working her first job during the school holidays. The name tag on her bib apron read Sally.

"You're doing a great job with that machine," Lilly told her and was rewarded with a huge smile. "It looks very complicated to me."

"It took a while to learn, but once you get the hang of it it's easy. It's nice to have the option for drinks now. I used to work on the pastry counter, but I prefer being here. Would you like chocolate sprinkles or powder?"

"Powder, please. I'm sorry, I didn't realise you'd been working here for a while. I thought you were new?"

"I've been here a couple of years now. I started as a Saturday girl. Now I work during school holidays when I can, too."

That would explain it. Lilly's Saturdays were spent at her own shop. She didn't come to The Loafer at the weekend, and only dropped of her produce every couple of months.

Lilly heard someone sigh behind her and realised a queue had started to form. She stepped to the side, intending to go back to her seat and wait for her coffee, when she saw a familiar face.

"Mirac?" she was surprised to see him. She'd assumed he'd be with Yasemin. She briefly considered asking him what had happened at the police station, but then thought better of it. It wasn't any of her business really, especially when it came to questioning someone who had been there. It would look very odd. Besides, she could always ask Bonnie if she really wanted to know.

Mirac glanced her way, looking slightly embarrassed. It had obviously been him sighing impatiently behind her. "Do I know you?"

Lilly was startled for a moment, then realised there was no reason why he would remember her. She felt as though she knew him because of what she had learned from Yasemin. But there was no reason why Yasemin should talk about Lilly in the same way to Mirac. She'd only really spoken to him once at the end of the night, and he was upset and confused because of the murder. She doubted he would be able to recall who had spoken to him.

"Not really," Lilly said now. "I did the catering for Edmund and Yasemin's wedding. I was there that night. I'm very sorry about Edmund, I know he was a close friend."

He nodded curtly. "It was shocking. I still can't believe it."

"Here's your drink," Sally said to Lilly, handing it over the counter.

Lilly thanked her and resumed her seat while waiting for Susanna. She was gazing out of the window at the busy street beyond when she heard Mirac shout. "How is it possible to get a simple order wrong?" before viciously throwing down the tub of spoons and storming out.

Lilly saw Sally's chin quiver slightly and her face flush the colour of beetroot. She was on the verge of tears. She left her drink on the counter and, after checking Sally was all right, charged out after Mirac.

"Mirac! Wait a minute. How dare you assault that poor girl? You need to apologise."

Mirac spun round, glaring at Lilly. He was probably expecting her to back down, but she stood her ground. There was no excuse for his behaviour and she was furious.

"I'll do no such thing. She's an idiot. How hard can it be to make a cup of coffee?" and with that, he spun on his heels and walked away.

*L*ILLY WATCHED HIM go, mouth agape. What on earth had just happened? She had pegged Mirac as being a calm and laid back sort of man. Obviously, she'd got that utterly wrong. She empathised with the fact he'd just lost a best friend in dreadful circumstances, but it didn't excuse his behaviour. However, he had been in a bad mood before entering the bakery. She wondered what had triggered his anger in the first place?

Back inside, the patrons had all gone quiet and Lilly could tell Sally was feeling humiliated.

"I didn't mean to upset him," she said, when Lilly went over to her. "He asked for soy milk and I used the normal stuff. I offered to make him a new one, but he got angry."

"It's not your fault, Sally. It was an easy mistake. But, it says much more about him than it does you. Try not to worry about it."

Susanna came back through to the shop carrying a large white paper bag with the bakery logo on the side.

"Is everything all right?" she asked, immediately sensing the tension.

"An angry customer," Lilly told her. "He was out of order, Susanna, it's not Sally's fault."

"Oh my goodness. Are you all right, Sally?"

"I'm fine. He was furious I used the wrong milk. I suppose it's my fault, really."

"It was a simple mistake, and you offered to rectify it. But his reaction was way over the top and borders on assault. Don't blame yourself. I can't believe he reacted so badly to not getting soy milk," Lilly said.

"Actually, it wasn't just that," Sally admitted. "The truth is I recognised him."

"Really?" Lilly asked. She didn't think Mirac would be a regular at The Loafer. He'd come specifically for the wedding and been here only a matter of days. Surely that wasn't long enough to get a bad reputation? But then again, she didn't know him and his short fuse had taken her by surprise. She supposed anything was possible.

"It was the same man who got into a fight here a couple of years ago. When he started being rude just now, I told him I remembered him because he had a bad attitude last time he was here. I hadn't been working here very long and it upset me. That's why I remember so clearly. I'm sorry, I shouldn't have said what I did."

Susanna rolled her eyes. "You mean the Turkish man?"

"Yes. And if it's all right with you, Susanna, I don't want to serve him again."

"Don't worry, Sally, no one will be serving him again. He's banned. Why don't you make yourself a drink and take a break? We can manage here."

Once Sally had left, Lilly turned to Susanna.

"His name is Mirac. I recently catered a wedding where he was the best man. So, he's caused problems here before?"

Susanna nodded. "Yes, he has. It was a couple of years ago, as Sally just told you. He was here with his wife visiting friends apparently and unfortunately bumped into one of her ex-boyfriends. This Mirac ended up punching the ex and knocked out one of his front teeth. It happened on the doorstep as they'd just left the shop and I saw it all. It was unwarranted and vicious, Lilly. It really was."

"It sounds as though he can't control his temper to me," Lilly said.

"And obviously very jealous where his wife is concerned," Susanna added.

Lilly didn't put her right about the subsequent divorce and remarriage of Mirac's former wife to his best friend. The news of the murder hadn't hit the papers yet. Bonnie must have been successful at putting some sort of gag order on Archie for the time being while she proceeded with the investigation.

After leaving the bakery, Lilly put the bread in her basket and contemplated her next move. She had intended to take care of some additional chores, but after seeing Mirac's behaviour, she decided to make a personal visit to Yasemin instead. She still needed to find a way to ask for the money she and Bethany were owed. This would be an ideal opportunity to kill two birds with one stone, she thought. Then winced inwardly at her chosen turn of phrase.

As she cycled through town on the way to Yasemin's hotel, her mind went back to the wedding and how obvious the love was between Edmund and Yasemin. Had Mirac been jealous, even though it was he who had introduced them and practically pushed them into the relationship? Then she remembered Stacey's comments. According to her, Mirac was still in love with Yasemin and possibly regretted the split. Was it actually Yasemin who'd instigated their parting rather than it being a joint decision? Could the reason have been because of Mirac's jealousy and temper? Lilly realised she had a lot of questions she'd like the answers to.

Mirac had just become suspect number one, as far as Lilly was concerned.

Chapter Eight

*L*ILLY CYCLED INTO the small car-park in front of the hotel and leaned her bike against the hedge. It was a former manor house on the outskirts of Plumpton Mallet, not exceptionally large, but catering to the affluent and therefore the height of luxury. The stables at the back of the main house had been converted into an indoor swimming pool and spa complex and, beyond that, were tennis courts. She knew Edmund and Yasemin had intended to stay a few days at the hotel after their marriage, with a honeymoon coming later in the year. But whether she had chosen to remain without him, she didn't know. Perhaps she should have phoned first, but a sixth sense told her to arrive unannounced. She pulled her phone from her pocket and rang Yasemin's number. She answered straight away.

"Lilly?"

"Hello, Yasemin. I'm outside your hotel and wondered if you felt up to a visit? Are you here?"

"Yes, I'm here. I'll let the concierge know to expect you. I'm in the..." she paused and exhaled shakily. Lilly realised she had about to say the honeymoon suite. "I'm in room two. Top floor."

"All right. I'll be there shortly."

The concierge nodded when she entered and indicated a beautiful replica of an old-fashioned bird cage lift in deep bronze. Lilly closed the gate and pressed the button for the top floor. She was pleased to have found Yasemin, but was concerned she was alone. With the newly married couple supposed to be on their honeymoon, she knew Esen had already returned home to Turkey. And obviously Mirac was in town. Perhaps it was as simple as Yasemin needing some space.

A moment later, she knocked on the door of room two and Yasemin greeted her. Her long dark hair was tied up with a silver barrette, but was damp from a recent shower and she looked fresh, dressed in crisp white jeans, navy blue loafers and a short-sleeved blue and white tee shirt. But she looked drained and her eyes were swollen and bloodshot and her nose red from crying. She closed the door behind Lilly and took one of the chairs in the bay window. Lilly sat in its twin opposite.

"I'm so sorry, Yasemin. How are you feeling? Is there anything I can do?"

Yasemin shook her head. "There's nothing. Unless you can bring Edmund back?" She twisted the platinum wedding band around her finger. "Do you know," she said so softly

Lilly could hardly hear her. "I've been Edmund's widow longer than I was his wife."

Lilly paused. "Yasemin, is there anyone you can stay with? I'm not sure it's a good idea you being on your own."

"There's no one here, really. Bruce offered, but I can't face going back there. And I'm sure you are aware Edmund's family didn't like me very much, but he said it didn't matter, they'd come around eventually when they saw how happy we were. But that was before I accused his Uncle Christopher. Now they've closed ranks and refuse to have anything to do with me. Perhaps I was out of line, I don't know."

"I don't think so, Yasemin. You were in dreadful shock, and out of everyone I would have thought his family would at least try to understand what you're going through. I'm sorry they are acting so poorly. What about your friends? Have you seen Mirac at all?"

"No. He sent me a text this morning to see how I was, but I haven't left this room since it happened, apart from speaking with the police. And it appears that I now have Edmund's debt to deal with."

"I thought his inheritance would cover that?" Lilly said.

"It would have done had he been alive. But his family is now saying I don't have a right to the money. We weren't married long enough. It's a legal nightmare. Naturally Christopher is going to fight it."

"His parents would have left him the money if they'd wanted him to have it," Lilly said. She wished she could say she was surprised by this development, but after seeing how Edmund's family had treated Yasemin, she wasn't.

"I don't know what to do. I feel as though I'm stuck in limbo. I can't do anything until the person who took Edmund's life is found and arrested. Lilly, I know I've already asked a lot from you, but will you help? I understand you've done something like this before?"

Lilly realised she'd already made a subconscious decision to investigate and found herself nodding at the request.

"Of course, I'll do what I can. In an unofficial capacity. My first suggestion is to find yourself a good solicitor. You need to have someone working on your behalf. Your in-laws are not going to make any of this easy for you, I'm afraid."

"Yes, I know. And I just don't have the energy to fight. I'll do as you say. Thank you."

"What about your mother and father? Can they come and be with you?"

Yasemin shook her head. "No, I've told them not to. They don't actually like to travel and to be honest, I don't think I can cope with all the arguments which are bound to happen if they do."

"All right, well if you need someone to talk to then you know where I am. It's one thing to have to face this with family and friends supporting you, quite another to have to do it on your own."

Yasemin reached across the small table and squeezed Lilly's hand, tears pooling in her eyes. "Thank you," she whispered. "Oh," she said rising. "I found this in my bag. I'm sorry I forgot to give it to you." She came back with a cheque for the outstanding amount owed for the catering and handed it to Lilly.

"Thank you, Yasemin. Are you sure?"

She waved her hand, dismissing Lilly's concern. "Yes, of course I am. You're owed for the job you did. Besides, it's only money. I can't bring myself to care about it now. I'd rather have my husband."

Lilly put the cheque in her own bag and asked Yasemin if she had eaten, to which she received a negative reply, so Lilly took it upon herself to order afternoon tea from room service. The sandwich selection was as luxurious as the venue; smoked salmon and cream cheese, Brie and watercress with a homemade fig pickle, turkey with avocado, sundried tomatoes and swiss cheese, and Lilly's personal favourite crab with avocado and lemon mayonnaise. Once they'd arrived, Lilly served them both and was pleased to see Yasemin eating, albeit daintily. With a cup of tea and a plate of food each, Lilly finally got around to discussing the real reason she'd come.

"HOW DID YOUR interview with the police go?" Lilly asked.

Yasemin shuddered. "It was horrible. All I could think about was poor Edmund. Your friend, the detective, asked me what happened. I couldn't tell her any more than what I told her at the reception. She asked if Edmund had any enemies and I said no. She then asked me the reason I accused Christopher. I told her about his mother's will. She made lots of notes, then said I was free to go but couldn't leave Plumpton Mallet. I'm innocent, Lilly, but what if she thinks I did this?"

Lilly shook her head. "It's normal procedure, Yasemin. If you're innocent, then you've nothing to worry about. Bonnie is just doing her job."

Lilly knew Bonnie would be looking into the background of all the concerned parties. Checking their whereabouts on the days leading up to the crime and on the day itself to ensure there were no anomalies. At the moment, everyone who had any connection to Edmund, no matter how tenuous, would be treated as a suspect until they could be alibied and eliminated. Unfortunately, as the spouse and with a hefty inheritance to gain, Yasemin would most likely be at the top of Bonnie's list. But she knew her friend well. She was excellent and diligent at her job. She would assume Yasemin to be innocent until she could prove without a shadow of a doubt she was guilty.

Personally, Lilly didn't think Yasemin had killed Edmund. But if not her, then who? And why?

"Have the police interviewed Mirac?" Lilly asked.

Yasemin eyed her cautiously. "Mirac? I don't know, but it cannot be him, Lilly. He was Edmund's best friend."

And you were his wife, Lilly thought, *but you were still interviewed.* "He's also your ex-husband and the circumstances of the relationship between the three of you are a little unorthodox, if you don't mind me saying so."

Lilly had to tread lightly. She didn't want to upset Yasemin more and run the risk of her shutting down completely. But Mirac had a vile temper which needed to be addressed.

"What are you suggesting?"

"That perhaps Mirac still has some serious feelings for you?"

To her surprise, Yasemin laughed. "No, not at all. What makes you think such a thing?"

Lilly took the opportunity to top up their tea while she gathered her thoughts.

"I was at The Loafer earlier, you know, the bakery in town and Mirac happened to be there. I witnessed him being abusive to one of the staff and when he left Susanna, the owner, told me about another incident he was involved in a couple of years ago."

Yasemin put her head in her hands. "I can't believe Mirac showed his face there again." She sighed, folded her arms and leaned back, gazing out of the window. "I know the incident she was referring to. We had come to Plumpton Mallet with Edmund, and were visiting with Bruce. It was while Mirac and I were still married, and long before Bruce inherited the estate. Outside the bakery, we bumped into an ex of mine, someone I had dated briefly before Mirac. We had gone on three or four dates, that's all. To the cinema, out for a meal or coffee, but nothing more. Unfortunately, to cut a long story short, he became very possessive, and I had to end it. He was angry and has hated me ever since. When we came across him here, he insulted me and my honour, Mirac defended me as a husband should. Yes, he punched him, but believe me, Lilly, he deserved it. In fact, to my mind, he deserved far more than Mirac actually gave him."

Lilly was surprise Yasemin found the incident perfectly acceptable. As far as she was concerned, assault was a serious matter and violence was never the answer. Lilly didn't know anything about the ex boyfriend, nor what he had said to make Mirac see red, but she was astounded Yasemin didn't care that Mirac had resorted to brutality. And by the sounds of it would have encouraged him to do more damage than he did. It left a sour taste in her mouth and for the first time, she found herself beginning to dislike Yasemin just a little.

"Mirac seems quite volatile. Does he lose his temper often?"

"Sometimes, but don't most men? He doesn't suffer fools gladly, but you cannot blame him for that. He's a successful, intelligent man."

"Are you sure Mirac doesn't still love you, Yasemin?"

"I know it looks odd from the outside, Lilly, and I agree it is a little unconventional, but you must believe Mirac and I are just friends. There is nothing between us and he would never hurt Edmund. It was Mirac who first mentioned the divorce, you know, not me. I wanted it every bit as much as he did, but I never brought it up until he shared with me how he felt. Mirac was not jealous of Edmund, if that's what you are implying. He was happy for both of us. I'm telling you, Christopher is the one who killed my husband."

Lilly still had her doubts, but she saw it was pointless to question Yasemin any further. She was adamant Mirac was innocent and Christopher guilty. Until evidence was found to the contrary, she would go on believing that.

She stood and made her excuses. She still had errands to run, but told Yasemin she could telephone anytime if she needed to talk.

She left the hotel feeling despondent, but sent a quick text to Bethany to say she'd got the cheque and once it had cleared from her bank, she'd send Bethany her half of the payment. Cycling out of the hotel gate, she went over her conversation with Yasemin. She hadn't found anything out that would help with the investigation and had unfortunately discovered Yasemin wasn't quite who she had thought she was. She sincerely hoped Bonnie was having better luck. She wanted this to be over as soon as possible.

Chapter Nine

*T*HE NEXT DAY, Lilly and Stacey were hard at work in the shop. They'd served a lot of customers, including a regular accompanied by his extended family who were visiting for a few days. They left with armfuls of tea, tea services and two of Lilly's favourite teapot designs; one shaped like an Indian elephant with the trunk as the spout, the tail as the handle and a cushion on his back, which served as the lid. The other an Alice in Wonderland design with the white rabbit holding his watch as the lid.

A moment after they'd left, the ringing shop bell signalled another customer. Stacey elbowed Lilly gently, and she looked up. To her surprise, it was Edmund's cousin Rachel. She looked pale and drawn.

"Rachel," Lilly said. "Please accept our condolences. We really are so sorry about what happened to Edmund."

Rachel nodded and took a seat at the counter. "Thank you. I can't believe he's gone. It just doesn't seem real. Who would do such a thing? I feel as though my family is falling apart and there's nothing I can do to stop it." She took a handkerchief from her bag and noisily blew her nose. "I'm sorry. I can't seem to stop crying."

"Don't worry. Is there anything I can do to help?"

"I was hoping you'd have something to help me sleep? Someone told me you were an expert on medicinal teas and I want to avoid sleeping tablets if possible. I can't function when I take them, they make me feel groggy and thick-headed. I've hardly slept since it happened. Every time I close my eyes, all I see is Edmund lying in a pool of blood."

"I've got several, which I'm sure will help, and I can brew a sample of them all for you to try so you can choose."

"What are they?"

Lilly began lifting boxes from the apothecary shelving display at the back of the counter and put them in front of Rachel, while Stacey sourced the same loose teas from the drawers for the samples and put the kettle on.

"Here we have Chamomile, Valerian Root, Lavender, Lemon Balm, Passion Flower, and Magnolia Bark. All of these will assist in helping you fall asleep faster, decrease nighttime awakenings and improve your overall quality of sleep. Sometimes a combination of one or more is a better option. I use Passionflower in conjunction with Valerian Root and hops if I'm suffering from a bout of insomnia for whatever reason. It also helps to reduce anxiety. Both of these have an earthy, grassy taste to them which personally

I like, but if you prefer something a bit sweeter, you can add natural honey."

By the time Lilly had finished explaining the benefits, Stacey had brewed the first two samples. Rachel took a tentative sip of the passion flower and nodded. "I quite like it." It was the same with the Valerian root. "Could you combine them with the hops like you suggested?" Stacey brewed a perfect blend for her and set aside some honey for sweetening just in case. But it wasn't necessary. "Yes, I like that much better. Could you pack me up a box?" Stacey nodded. "I hope it works," Rachel said. "I don't feel as though I'll ever sleep again. First Ellie disappeared and now Edmund is dead."

"What happened to Edmund's sister?" Lilly asked. She'd been curious ever since she'd found out about her.

"She fell in love," Rachel scoffed. "Unfortunately, he was the wrong sort, if you get my meaning."

Lilly didn't exactly, but she felt Stacey stiffen beside her.

"NOT QUITE. WHAT do you mean?" she asked. "He was not one of us. And he was from the wrong side of town, too. Ellie was too good for him, but of course she couldn't see it. Personally, I never understood why she would want to be with someone who was quite obviously beneath her. The only thing that could have made it worse was if he'd been a servant as well. Thank goodness for small mercies. The family would never have lived that down. I suppose I'm partially to blame for Ellie leaving. I told her in no uncertain terms that she should break up with him. He wasn't our sort, and the family would never accept him. I mean, could you blame us, really?" she said with a conspiratorial smile at Lilly. "And I was right. They backed me and told her he came from a different background and their union would neither be blessed by them, nor would it ever work."

Out of the corner of her eye, Lilly noticed Stacey moving away from the counter toward the back of the shop. It was unusual behaviour, as Stacey loved a bit of gossip normally. She kept a concerned eye on her while Rachel continued, but had a sinking feeling she now knew exactly what Rachel was alluding to.

"Ellie threatened to leave. All very dramatic and pointless. And I told her to stay. Told her she was a fool for choosing that sort over her own family and she'd live to regret it. She was gone the next day. Left no note and we haven't seen or heard from her since."

"Did you look for her?"

"Me? No, of course not. She made her own bed. None of the family did except Edmund. He was terribly upset she'd gone without a word. I mean, she was his sister, so it's understandable, I suppose. He told us we'd behaved very poorly toward her, although in hindsight he never aligned himself with her. I don't think he ever found her. Or at least he never told us if he did. And then would you believe he did the same thing as Ellie? Fell in love with Yasemin. At least to my credit, I handled their relationship better than I did Ellie's."

Lilly glanced at Stacey and raised her eyebrows. If Rachel called what she did to Yasemin better, then she could only imagine the hell she'd put Edmund's sister through.

"When Edmund came home with Yasemin," Rachel continued. "The family were mortified. How could he bring a girl of that character to the house and declare they were to marry? Someone even asked if she was applying for a position as a maid," Rachel laughed. "I mean, it was funny, but I told them to at least try to give her a chance. We didn't want a repeat of what happened with Ellie."

"And did they?" Lilly asked through gritted teeth.

Rachel sighed. "Well they tried. As did I. We really did, but they came from different worlds. It would never have worked in the long run."

Lilly could see Stacey was beginning to get very agitated and was about to suggest she take a break when Rachel spoke again.

"All I wanted was for Edmund to stay in the family and find someone who was worthy of him. Just like I wanted for Ellie."

Then the damn broke and Stacey could no longer hold back.

"**W**ORTHY?" SHE SHOUTED. "You mean someone who was white, don't you? You know it's people like you..." she stopped and took a deep breath. "I mean, can you even hear yourself? It's you and your family who are not worthy of Yasemin and whoever Ellie's boyfriend was. You know if we all took off our skin, we'd look exactly the same, right? You're just racist and intolerant. You make me sick."

83

"How dare you speak to me like that," Rachel said in fury. "Are you just going to stand there and let a simple shop girl insult me like that?" she said, turning to Lilly.

"Yes, actually, I am. I happen to agree with everything she said. And she's not a simple shop girl, as you so offensively put it. She's one of the brightest, smartest and personable people I have ever met. And I'm very lucky to have her. Now, I think you should leave," Lilly said.

"Leave? Whatever for? I haven't done anything."

"If I have to explain, then you'll never understand. Now, please go or I'll call the police and have you forcibly removed, Rachel."

"As if they'd take you seriously. I've committed no crime."

"No, but I happen to have a friend who is a detective. I'm sure we can think of something."

"Don't be so ridiculous. Don't worry, this is not the sort of place I want to shop, anyway."

"Luckily, this is my business and you're not the sort of person I wish to serve, either." Lilly responded calmly.

After Rachel had stormed out, slamming the door in her wake and frightening Earl, who jumped out of his basket in the window and scarpered to the back room, Lilly found herself on the receiving end of a fierce hug.

"Crikey. What was that for?"

"For supporting me and taking my side," Stacey said tearfully. Although Lilly knew they were tears borne of anger and frustration rather than distress.

"Of course I did, Stacey. I'll always support you, especially in front of customers and even if you're wrong. But you weren't. How did you know so quickly that she was discriminating because of race?"

"Because I grew up hearing those phrases. My step dad is African American, and he's the nicest guy you could ever know. He practically raised me and was the best step-father ever. You should have heard the things our neighbours and the kids at school said about him. I got in a couple of fights because of it. When you grow up hearing it all the time, it sticks. It makes me so mad."

"I'm not surprised. It would make me mad too. I'm sorry you and your family had to deal with such narrow-minded prejudice. You know, I didn't realise how bad in that regard Edmund's family was. I heard recently that it was possible, but I always try to see the best in people until they prove otherwise. Well, Rachel and people like her are not welcome in my shop."

"Thanks, Lilly. Oh, she took the tea!"

"Well, we did blend it for her."

"Yes, but she never paid for it."

"Oh, I see. Well, never mind, Stacey. It's only tea. A small price to pay for getting rid of her."

"We could always get Bonnie to arrest her for shoplifting," Stacey said, laughing.

"I don't think we need to go that far. There's no point wishing bad things for her." Lilly said with a smile.

"Oh, I don't know. Besides, I'm not sure I can help myself."

"Tell me, Stacey, are you happy?"

"What?" the girl asked, surprised at the sudden change in the conversation.

"Are you happy?"

"Yes, I am."

"Why?"

"I have a wonderful family. I have a great job. My boss is the best," she added with a grin. "I love college. I have loads of brilliant friends and a fab boyfriend. And me and my dad are really getting on well."

Lilly nodded. "And what about Rachel? Do you think she's happy?"

"Rachel? No way. She looks pretty miserable actually, and she's really uppity. Thinks she's better than everyone else. And she's racist."

"Exactly. With that much hatred in her heart, she'll never be happy, Stacey. We don't need to wish her ill. She's doing very well on her own."

"Wow! No wonder you're such a good agony aunt," Stacey said.

Lilly laughed. "And here endeth today's lesson."

The rest of the day went smoothly with a lot of sales and a number of new customers. By closing time, both Lilly and Stacey were tired and glad of the day's end. They made short work of tidying up and preparing for the next day, then Lilly handed Stacey an envelope.

"What's this?"

"It's a thank you for all the work you did for the wedding. I seriously couldn't have done it without you."

Stacey peered in the envelope and looked at Lilly with wide eyes. "This is way too much," she said.

"You earned it. Between helping me with the catering, running the shop while I was out so much, and for getting the job in the first place, you deserve every penny."

Stacey was beside herself and thanked Lilly profusely, and for the second time that day gave her a hug. It was a happy end to what had turned out to be a very trying day. Let's hope tomorrow is better, Lilly said to herself.

Chapter Ten

*L*ILLY WENT INTO work a bit later the next day, as Stacey had offered to open the shop. She spent the extra hour taking care of numerous household chores that had been neglected due to the time she'd spent working on Edmund and Yasemin's wedding, while Earl snoozed in his basket by the unlit fire.

Eventually, with the cottage hoovered, dusted and polished to within an inch of its life, and the washing done and hung on the airer to dry, she scooped up her cat and put him in his carrier. With a final look round, she locked up, placed the cat carrier in the basket of her bike and set off to work.

As she arrived outside the shop, she could see Stacey talking animatedly with a customer about the latest selection of teapots which had arrived, while two others were drinking samples and another was wandering around browsing the displays.

"We're here, Earl," she said to the cat, lifting the carrier out and leaving her bike outside ready to decorate. Inside, she unzipped the carrier and Earl strolled out in his regular lazy fashion, stretching his legs and yawning before hopping up into the window and resuming his nap. He was certainly making up for the time he lived by his wits on the street. *He can't have got much sleep then*, Lilly thought, *and no doubt slept with one eye open*. She assumed this was where the term 'cat nap' came from.

After checking the agony aunt basket and finding two new letters, Lilly took her place behind the counter just in time to take payment from a customer Stacey had been helping.

"Did you find everything you came for?" she asked the elderly woman.

"Oh, I did, dear. And a few things I didn't know I needed," she said, giving a toothy smile. "Your young American girl was very kind and helpful. And knew so much."

Lilly returned the smile. People were always amazed that the American college student she'd hired knew so much about British tea. "She's one of a kind," Lilly said, wrapping the order carefully. The woman left happy with her purchases and with promises to return with the members of her knitting club.

"Lilly, I had a telephone order for a loose tea earlier. I've wrapped it up ready," Stacey said, reaching under the counter and retrieving a large box wrapped in The Tea Emporium paper and with a thank you for your purchase tag attached to the jute ribbon. "It's a tourist, I think. He's staying at The Wharfe B&B and asked if we could deliver? I said yes since it's so close. Is that okay?"

"Of course it is. It's in the park, so only a five minute bike ride away. What room number is he in?"

"5b."

"Okay, thanks, Stacey. I'll take it now while it's a bit quieter."

The B&B was actually on Lilly's route home, but instead of turning right at the bottom of the hill in the park, she went left. Cycling under the avenue of cherry trees, now in their autumn coat, she was in the car-park a couple of minutes later.

Inside, she went to the reception desk and asked if she could leave the delivery for room 5b.

"Oh, actually," the receptionist said. "The gentleman has asked if you would deliver them personally? It's on the next floor. Turn right at the top of the stairs. You can't miss it."

Lilly was surprised, but was intrigued as to who the customer was so took the stairs as instructed. Room 5b was down a small hall with a clean but dated carpet, and prints of old local scenes in dark wood frames. She knocked on the door and waited.

"Oh, excellent, you've brought my tea," Christopher Rogers said to a startled Lilly when he flung open the door. "Come in and I'll put the kettle on. You'll stay for a cup, will you?"

Lilly hesitated for a fraction of a second before agreeing. Both Stacey and the receptionist knew exactly where she was. Plus the B&B was so small if she needed to scream, she'd be heard immediately. Besides, this was the perfect opportunity to do a bit of sleuthing.

"You obviously liked my teas, then?"

"I did. I tried all your special blends at the wedding. Before I was dragged out by the police, of course. I spoke with your assistant this morning. A very smart girl. Knew exactly what I was talking about." He opened the box and examined the contents before nodding in approval. "Yes, this is the stuff. I wanted to make sure I got some before I left."

"You're leaving Plumpton Mallet?" Lilly asked. She was surprised considering he was a suspect in a murder case and she'd heard Bonnie expressly say that no one was to leave.

"It's not as though I live here," he replied with a shrug. "I live in London, but have been forced to stay here because apparently there's no room at Bruce's." He rolled his eyes. "He just didn't want me there in case I rock the boat more like it."

"No offense, but from the outside looking in, it seems like a valid argument," Lilly said and Christopher laughed.

"I suppose so. But believe me, I'm not the only one in the family. And I'd never hurt my nephew no matter what anybody thinks. I'm as upset as anyone that he's gone. More probably."

He added the boiling water to the tea pot and let it steep for a few minutes before pouring it through the strainer Stacey had included in the box, and handing Lilly her cup.

"It's a pity you don't sell those cocktails of yours, too. I'd have bought the lot if you did."

"I'd need an alcohol license for those," she said. But made a mental note to explore the possibility in the future. "So, when are you leaving?"

"As soon as the police say I can. Hopefully it won't be too long now, considering I had nothing to do with it. That girl Yasemin really got me into trouble by pointing the finger at me like she did."

Lilly nodded. "Had you met her before the wedding?"

Christopher shook his head, indicating she should take the single seat in the room while he perched on the edge of the bed. "No. A lot of the extended family hadn't. Mind you, I can't say I blame Edmund for not introducing her after what happened with Ellie."

"I've never met Ellie. She wasn't at the wedding."

"No one has seen her in years. Ran out when they took a disliking to her boyfriend. I'm ashamed to be part of the family because of that. I didn't agree with their stance, although I admit I've caused more than my fair share of drama over the years. Particularly where my niece and nephew were concerned."

"What do you mean?" Lilly asked. She was pleasantly surprised at how verbose Christopher Rogers was being, so played ignorant in the hope she'd learn something new or useful for Bonnie. Then she realised the very reason he could have invited her in was because he knew she and Bonnie were friends. Was he trying to pull the wool over her eyes in the hope she'd report back to her detective friend? Perhaps. She decided she'd push a little, but take what he said with a pinch of salt.

CHRISTOPHER EXHALED LOUDLY. "I suppose it all started when Edmund and Ellie's parents died. Losing my older brother and his wife hit me hard. Very hard. Edmund and Ellie were just kids, so my parents took them in. Looking back, I can see it was the right thing to do. The only thing, but I was pretty young myself and to see the two of them get so much attention... well, I suppose I was jealous. I'm not proud of it. I should have handled it better than I did. But there it is. I left home as soon as I could and never looked back. I turned up once in a while, mainly for holidays or birthdays, but eventually it was just easier to stay away and get on with my life. I'll admit in the latter years it was Edmund and Ellie who took care of my parents, but I never thought they'd write me out of the will."

"So with one son having passed away and the other cutting ties with them, they raised their grandchildren on their own," Lilly said with a touch of sarcasm. "And consequently left everything to them in their will."

"Basically," he nodded and shrugged, apparently bewildered. Lilly was stunned he couldn't see the obvious.

"Are you intending to contest the will? By rights half of it, if not all depending on how long Ellie has been missing and if your mother changed the will in Edmund's favour once it was apparent she wouldn't be coming back, will go to Yasemin now Edmund is dead won't it?"

"I don't think that's any of your business," Christopher said, frowning. "Yasemin was married to Edmund for a matter of hours. My parents didn't leave the money to her they left it to Edmund and his sister. Ellie's been missing for years and Edmund is dead. Don't you think their own son has more claim on that money than some foreign girl Edmund knew for a year or so at best?"

"What are you going to do if Ellie does suddenly turn up?" Lilly asked. "Would you fight her for it if she was still in the picture?"

"I don't have to worry about that. She doesn't want anything to do with the family. She's not going to come out of the woodwork now. It's been far too long."

Lilly finished her tea and handed her cup and saucer into Christopher's outstretched hand. He moved to the small sideboard and stacked them on the tray.

"I spoke with Rachel recently," Lilly said, as Christopher sat back down. "I'm under the impression she had quite a bit to do with Ellie leaving in the first place."

"She had everything to do with it. Look, if you've talked to Rachel, then you'll know the real reason Ellie's boyfriend wasn't considered good enough." Lilly nodded. "Well, what you may not know is Ellie's boyfriend left her, citing the family's ignorance and prejudice as the reason. Mainly because Rachel was so vocal about it."

Lilly shook her head. "No, I didn't know that. How awful for her."

"I agree. But you can't blame the man. He would never have been accepted and was actively disliked within the family purely because... well, you know. But it wasn't just Rachel, she was the loudest, that's all. To cut a long story short, Rachel and Ellie got into a huge argument at a function which caused a rift in the family. Some agreed with Ellie, but most took Rachel's side. Ellie left and none of us have heard from her since. Everyone gives me a hard time, but at least I show up on occasion. Ellie completely vanished."

"It seems to me as though Ellie didn't get the support she needed," Lilly said. "Look, it's none of my business, but how do you think your brother would have felt knowing his family fell apart? As their uncle, you could have stepped up, you know? They are your brother's children."

Christopher stood up suddenly. So as not to be at a disadvantage and not knowing what to expect, Lilly did the same and made sure to take a couple of steps closer to the door. "You're right, it's none of your business," he snarled at her. "And I'm not going to listen to you judge me about a situation you know very little about. I think it's time you left."

"Yes, I think so too," Lilly replied, moving toward the door. "Enjoy your tea."

"I didn't want anything to happen to my nephew, Miss Tweed. I know there's plenty of people who think I did because of the inheritance, but they can think what they want. I'm innocent and sooner or later the police are going to realise I am too."

Lilly smiled, nodded politely, and left. Outside, she mounted her bike and began the return journey to the shop, wondering why Christopher Rogers had insisted she have tea with him? As far as she could determine, it was simply a ploy to try and persuade her of his innocence. She made a mental note to email Bonnie about it. No doubt this is what Christopher had intended. But perhaps he protested a little too much?

*L*ILLY HAD JUST stopped at the main road and was waiting for a lull in the traffic so she could cross, when her phone buzzed to signify a text. She took one look at it and burst out laughing. It was from Archie. She called him back.

"Learning how to use emojis, are we?" she giggled when he answered.

"I thought I'd give it a go, yes. Why? What are you laughing at?"

"What were you trying to say, Archie?"

"I wondered if you had time to meet up for a coffee?"

"Yes, I understood that much, but what about the rest of it?"

"A bun. Coffee and a bun or a whatchamacallit, a cupcake, or something."

"Oh, Archie," Lilly said, trying and failing not to laugh again.

There was a lengthy silence while Archie waited for her to control herself.

"So, it's obviously not a bun. What does it mean, then?"

"It means poop."

"It does not! Good grief, who invented this nonsense? I suppose you're going to tell me the peach one doesn't mean peach cobbler, aren't you?"

"Archie, stop! I can't breathe," Lilly said, guffawing loudly and causing several drivers to stare in astonishment.

"So do you want to meet for a coffee?"

"Yes."

"And a bun?"

"Absolutely. As long as it's not chocolate."

Archie snorted. "You'll get what you're given and be grateful for it. I'll meet you at the coffee shop across the road from the paper."

"Okay, I'll be there in ten minutes."

She hung up and sent a quick text to Stacey informing her of the change in the plan, then pushed her bike across the road, her sides still aching from laughing at Archie's faux pas. She'd better ask Stacey to train him in emoji 101.

Archie was already sitting at a table in the back of the coffee shop when she arrived. He looked up and lifted his hand. "Don't say a word. I don't want to talk about it."

Lilly grinned. "My lips are sealed. Have you ordered?"

"Two cappuccinos and a slice of cake each. Not chocolate before you ask, coffee and walnut."

"That's perfect, Archie. So, do you have news?" she asked, leaning back as the waitress served their coffees and cake with a cheery smile.

"I heard from Bonnie last night," he said, clasping his mug in two hands and leaning forward so she could hear when he dropped his voice. "There's absolutely no forensics to be found on the murder weapon at all. No prints, no DNA. Nothing."

"Seriously?" Lilly said, and Archie nodded. "I can't believe it. I felt sure they'd find something considering the knife was so carelessly left by the body." Lilly shook her head, imagining how stressed poor Bonnie must be feeling. She was still new to her role as lead detective and Lilly knew she put a lot of pressure on herself to perform well. She'd give her a call later to see how she was doing.

"The killer was obviously very lucky. It's as rare as hen's teeth to find nothing on a murder weapon. They might have been wearing gloves, but I don't remember anyone at the wedding with gloves, do you?" Lilly shook her head. "Well, the police are now interviewing everyone again, double checking time-lines and alibis and whatnot hoping to shake something loose. It's good old fashioned detective work but time consuming." Archie said. "Anyway, you're a smart woman, Lilly, and I thought I'd pick your brains for the articles I'm writing."

"With a compliment like that, how could I refuse, Archie. Shall we talk it through? What are your thoughts so far?"

"WELL, THE OBVIOUS one is Yasemin. The inheritance Edmund was going to receive was apparently quite hefty, so it's a prime motive. I've no idea how much it's worth, but the family were certainly gossiping about it at the wedding, so it's certainly enough to encourage jealous whispers. Plus, she's the spouse, and that's where the police tend to look first."

"Mmm, maybe," Lilly said. "She was certainly the one physically closest to Edmund when it happened. She was standing right next to him when the lights went out and was still there when they came back on. Only this time, she was covered in his blood. Of course, she knelt down and held him, so it's easy to explain how that happened. Although, she could have done that to disguise the splashes of blood she received from stabbing him in the first place."

Archie took another mouthful of coffee and sighed appreciatively, before turning back to the conversation. "Don't you think it's a bit suspicious she's claiming she didn't see anything? I know it was dark, but still, you'd have thought she'd have seen or at least felt something when she was so close to the victim, wouldn't you? I know she said they stepped apart for a moment when it went dark, but how can we know for sure? There's only her word."

"There's also the debt," Lilly said. "Right before the ceremony, Yasemin found out Edmund had been keeping a massive debt from her. It was the reason she very nearly called off the wedding. We're not talking a few hundred pounds here, Archie, it runs into thousands. Maybe she was more angry about it than I realised? But then again, killing him would only mean she'd be saddled with owing the money. Perhaps she did it thinking she'd get the inheritance which would take care of the debt, but hadn't banked on Christopher Rogers contesting it and trying to lay claim to it himself? I'm just thinking out loud here, Archie. I'm not convinced Yasemin is our killer yet."

"It does seem a very risky thing to do," Archie said. "Perhaps too risky? She knew Christopher was bitter and angry that Edmund was listed as the heir. It seems highly likely he would pursue the money. Yasemin is involved enough for me not to write her off completely, but at this point, I don't really believe she's the culprit. Do you?"

Lilly shook her head. "No, not really. The two of them were genuinely in love. It was obvious to anyone who saw them together. I agree she should go on the 'possible' pile for now."

"Well, there's certainly a slew of others who are just as likely and more than capable of committing this crime," Archie said.

"Yes. Mirac for one." Lilly said.

"Ah, yes. The ex-husband. Is it me or is that whole situation strange? I honestly don't know of anyone who would agree to be the best man to the groom who was marrying your ex-wife. Unless he was there purely to get rid of the competition? That's the obvious motive, but why not just stay married to her in that case? Do you want another coffee, Lilly? I think we could be here a while discussing this?"

Lilly said she would, so Archie cleared the table, took their china back to the counter and ordered another two cappuccinos. He paid and waited to bring them back with him, chatting easily with the server. Lilly took the opportunity to send a quick email to Bonnie, updating her on the conversations she'd had with the 'players' so far, telling her where she was and the fact she was having a 'pow-wow' with Archie. She received a brief, 'OK, thanks,' in reply. Obviously, she was busy.

"You know, I talked to Mirac at the reception and he'd had quite a bit to drink," Archie said as he returned and sat down.

"Drowning his sorrows, do you think?" Lilly asked.

"Very possibly. He's not really a drinker from what I gather, so whatever he had hit him hard. Possibly your fabulous cocktails," he added with a wink. "Do you think it could have been him? A spur-of-the-moment decision brought on in anger because of the alcohol?"

"He's certainly got a temper without having a drink, so it's as good an idea as any."

"If he did do it, he's lucky he didn't get covered in blood. Bonnie and her team were quick off the mark and thoroughly checked everyone as soon as they arrived. Only Yasemin had any blood on her."

"I suppose Mirac could be jealous," Lilly said. "Stacey certainly seemed to think so, but Yasemin was adamant it was he who instigated the divorce process."

"Perhaps that was just to keep her happy?" Archie suggested.

"He was certainly quick to offer a shoulder to cry on. And he insisted he be the one to take her to the police station for her interview rather than Esen."

"Do you think his feelings for her are strong enough to kill his best friend, thus leaving the way clear to get her back?" Archie asked, spooning brown sugar into his coffee and stirring thoughtfully.

Lilly shrugged. "He hasn't voiced his feelings, but if anyone's got the temperament, it's him."

"Yes, you mentioned a temper. How do you know?"

"I witnessed him in The Loafer going off the deep end because he got the wrong milk in his coffee. Then Susanna told me about another incident." She relayed the information to Archie, who raised his eyebrows and shook his head. "Perhaps," she continued. "Seeing them so happy together stirred up feelings he didn't realise he had? The knife was from a nearby table, so it was close to hand. To my mind, there doesn't seem to be a lot of planning to this crime, Archie. Maybe, fueled by alcohol, he just saw red and killed

Edmund in a fit of anger, then realising what he'd done, he dropped the knife and got out of the way before the lights came back on?"

"Yes, that's more than possible. And if it wasn't Mirac, then the same could apply to any of the others. Interesting."

"Including Rachel. She's racist to the core, Archie, and didn't hide how much she disliked Yasemin."

"But if that was the case, wouldn't it make more sense for her to do away with the bride rather than her own cousin?"

"Yes, but what if that actually was her plan but Edmund got in the way? It was dark, remember."

"Good grief, Lilly! Could throw a bigger spanner in the works?" Archie said, laughing. He sat back and folded his arms, thinking seriously about what she'd suggested for a short while before shaking his head. "I can't see it. Even in the dark, I don't think you'd mix up the two of them. Purely by what they were wearing, if nothing else. Whoever killed Edmund was going after him, I'm almost sure of it."

"Okay. So you think we can eliminate Rachel as a suspect then?"

"We'll put her on the 'not very likely' pile for now. Which leaves good old Uncle Christopher."

"I was just leaving him when you sent me your text, Archie. He bought some of my tea and insisted I not only deliver it, but share a cup when I got there."

"Oh? Well, that sounds suspicious. What did he want?"

Lilly relayed the whole conversation.

"So it was an excuse to vent his spleen a bit and make sure you passed on to Bonnie how innocent he is? That sounds very typical of the man, if you ask me. Well, he certainly has a motive, feeling he was cheated out of inheritance. He goes on the highly possible pile."

"This is exhausting, Archie. I feel like we're going round in circles. I still keep coming back to the lack of blood on the culprit and absolutely no clues whatsoever on the murder weapon. I hope Bonnie is having more luck."

"I don't think she is, Lilly."

"How do you know?"

"Because she's just walked in. And I think she wants to pick our brains."

Chapter Eleven

ONNIE WAVED, THEN went straight to the counter and ordered a large black coffee with a Danish pastry, bringing them over to their table and slumping into the seat next to Lilly.

"I really hope you two have got some additional insight into this murder, which is alluding me. Because so far it's a nightmare."

Lilly could see how much this case was weighing on her friend's shoulders. Bonnie was an excellent detective and worked harder at her job than anyone she knew. But she was Plumpton Mallet's first female principal detective. Consequently, she was in the spotlight and with a lot of eyes on her, most wanting her to succeed but a very small minority were waiting for her to fail.

"Are you all right, Bonnie?" Archie asked, concern etched on his face.

"Hanging on by a thread, Archie. I need to find some answers, and quickly, otherwise I could find myself demoted. So, what are you two amateur sleuths discussing? Have you found out anything useful?"

"We're just rehashing what we know to see if I can get a decent initial article together," Archie replied. "There's not much to go on apart from the obvious, and that doesn't paint you lot in a good light, I'm afraid. Do you have anything new to add since we last spoke?"

"Nothing. We haven't been able to narrow it down much further than the night it happened."

"You really don't have anything at all you could tell us?" Lilly asked.

"I really don't. We're chasing our tales on this blasted case and it's beyond frustrating. So far, in interviews, we've covered every motive you can think of; love, hate, jealousy, money, and we even considered killing Edmund was a mistake. That he wasn't the intended victim at all, but his wife was."

Lilly nodded. "Yes, I came up with that as a possibility, but Archie said it was unlikely. Having thought about it, I agree with him."

"We came to that conclusion as well," Bonnie said. "To be honest we're stumped... and I'd appreciate you not quoting me on that, Archie, when the time comes to print."

"I wouldn't do that Bonnie."

"How did the interviews with the family members go?" Lilly asked.

Bonnie scoffed. "Exactly as you would expect. Every one of them has an alibi."

"They do?" Lilly and Archie asked at the same time.

"Oh, yes. It's like this; Family member A swore they were standing next to family member B the entire time. Before, during, and after the lights went off and on. Family member B says the same thing. With me so far?" Lilly and Archie nodded. "Good. But neither family member A or family member B mentioned family member C. So I interview family member C and they state they were with family members A and B all the time. So being the diligent detective I am, I re-interview family members A and B and would you believe it, they both suddenly say, 'oh, yes, how silly of me, I remember now, family member C was standing next to me.' The same goes for the rest of them."

"So they're all just alibiing each other?" Lilly said.

"Yes. Now you can see what I'm up against. One or all of them could be lying, but I can't tell who. I doubt any of this would hold up in court, but they are all claiming they didn't see anything. I need to break these alibis if I'm going to get to the truth."

"How will you do that?" Archie asked.

"We started by creating a floor plan based on what everyone said during their interviews, trying to work out who was close enough to the bride and groom to have done it. But we soon discovered it wasn't going to work. You know how disoriented you feel when you're in the dark? You start off in one place, then the lights go out and you start to move. When the lights come back on, you're in a different place to where you started, but with no clear idea of the route you took to get there, nor who you bumped into on the way. Plus, the lights were actually off long enough for someone to get onto the dance floor, stab the victim, drop the knife, and get back in plenty of time to stand with the person, giving them the alibi. I tried it, so I know. It doesn't matter who it is, nor if that's where you actually were before the lights failed, as long as you're far enough away from the crime."

"Oh my gosh, Bonnie," Lilly said. "How on earth are you going to unravel this mess? It's obvious the family isn't cooperating. I wonder why?"

"Let me get another coffee and I'll let you know what I think," Bonnie replied, standing and walking back to the counter.

"She doesn't look well, does she?" Archie said.

"She's pushing herself too hard. I know she wants a fast result, as do her superiors, but it's only been a matter of days, Archie. No one can be expected to solve a murder case that quickly. If she keeps on the way she is, then she'll end up being ill. Then she won't be able to work at all. We need to help her."

"Of course we do. And we will, Lilly. Let's change the subject. She's coming back."

"RIGHT," BONNIE SAID, taking her seat. "Where was I?"

"The reason the family isn't cooperating," Archie said.

Bonnie nodded. "I think it's because of what happened to Edmund's sister years ago. You've seen the way they go at one another. There's no trust between them. The family is hanging on by a thread. None of them want to say or do anything that will feed the fire again and cause either resentment or another rift. It appears they've decided to rally together and ensure none of them gets accused."

"So they're all bending the truth a little, meaning you can't get a realistic picture of what happened?" Lilly said.

"Exactly. It's so frustrating. Then when the knife came back and there was nothing on it at all? Well... I'm beginning to wonder if I should just throw in the towel and have done with it. I mean we're still conducting interviews, but to be honest they're not going anywhere."

"You don't think Yasemin was responsible?"

Bonnie shook her head. "No I don't, Lilly. I've investigated that angle thoroughly. She had nothing to gain except a massive debt and what will amount to a bitter, costly and lengthy court battle against Christopher for gain of the inheritance. And even then, she might not win. Then she'd have huge costs to pay on top of the debt Edmund has left her with. She doesn't strike me as the sort of person to take that risk. Also, the timing doesn't make sense. If she wanted him dead, she would have had ample opportunity to do it at a later date and make it look like an accident. You don't choose to kill your new spouse at the wedding in front of so many witnesses. It doesn't make sense."

"When you put it like that, I think you're right," Lilly said.

"There's a part of me wonders if whoever did this wanted to make Yasemin look guilty, though," Bonnie said. "They just did a very bad job of it and didn't think it through properly. If at all. By the same token, it could have been an opportunity they couldn't pass up when the lights went out. As far as I'm concerned, Yasemin doesn't have a strong enough motive, but there are others who do. Mirac, Christopher and Rachel to start with. Although I don't believe Mirac would try to blame Yasemin, I think the others would."

"We were both talking about that very point as it pertains to cousin Rachel before you came in, actually," Lilly said. "We put her on the 'not likely to have committed this crime' pile. If her issue was not wanting Yasemin to marry her cousin because of race, she wouldn't have killed Edmund. It would have been Yasemin she'd target. I'll admit she's not a very nice person, but she isn't stupid or unhinged enough to have done this."

"Mmm, I'm not so sure, Lilly," Bonnie said. "She is domineering and manipulative, the epitome of a control freak, as Stacey would call her, especially when it comes to her family. I mean, look what happened to the sister. She cut herself off from the whole family in order to escape the prejudice and influence of them all, but especially Rachel. Perhaps Rachel killed Edmund when she realised he wasn't going to bow to her demands, therefore, according to how she saw it, tainting the family reputation and bloodline?"

Lilly didn't believe that was the case, but all of them were grasping at straws at this moment in time, and any and all explanations deserved to be thrown into the pot in the first instance. You never knew what initial idea or off-the-cuff comment, no matter how speculative, would develop into something worth pursuing and ultimately solve the case.

"I can't help thinking about the murder weapon," Lilly said.

"What do you mean?" Bonnie asked.

"The buffet was laid just prior to the first guests arriving, so no later than seven o'clock. It was only available for an hour and by nine o'clock everyone had finished eating and nearly half of the clearing away had been done by the catering staff. No one was hanging around the buffet table. I had a clear view from the bar. And the small number of sit down tables at the edge of the room were cleared first. We made those a priority to prevent accidents because they were the closest to the dance floor. We know the knife was part of the catering cutlery set, so it was taken at some point from a table. The question is when? I believe the person who killed Edmund must have already had the knife on them before the lights went out."

Both Bonnie and Archie glanced at one another in sudden understanding, then looked back at Lilly.

"Well done, Lilly," Archie said.

"Yes, that's a very good point. Excuse the unintentional pun," Bonnie agreed. "If they had the knife on them, it meant they knew they were going to have an opportunity to kill Edmund. Which meant they also knew the lights were going to go out. This wasn't an opportunistic murder at all. It was premeditated."

"**D**ID YOUR LOT find anything when you went to check the fuse box, Bonnie?" Archie asked. "Nothing. But of course, we didn't arrive until the lights were back on. I questioned Bruce personally, and he said the fuse switch for the ballroom had flipped off, so he just flipped it back on and everything worked normally. It's quite an old system because of the age of the house, so he thought it might be damp that had caused a short-circuit somewhere. The fuse box is housed in the cellars, so below ground level, which makes it more than feasible."

"Well, now it's almost certain the killer deliberately turned the lights off," Lilly said. "Although I've no idea how we'll prove that. Is there anything else you can tell us, Bonnie?"

Bonnie looked down, idly stirring her coffee for a moment. "All right, there is one thing," she said finally, looking up. "And, Archie, I need your solemn promise this won't appear in the paper until I say it can. We're deliberately holding this information back."

"You know I would never publish anything without your permission, Bonnie," Archie assured her. "But you've certainly piqued my interest. What is this secret snippet you talk of, dear detective?"

"We found a note in the deceased's jacket pocket. It said, and I quote; *'We need to talk. Meet me in the rose garden before the ceremony.'*"

"Who wrote it?" Lilly asked.

"We don't yet. It obviously wasn't signed, but we've eliminated Yasemin. It's not a match for her handwriting regardless of whether she uses her left or her right hand, or if she tries to disguise it."

"It could be something totally innocent," Lilly said. "A surprise gift for Yasemin, for example."

"Of course it could. But this is a murder inquiry and at the moment I am treating everything as suspicious."

"Do you know if Edmund actually met with this mystery note writer?" Archie asked.

Bonnie let out an exasperated sigh. "No, not yet. But I intend to get hand writing samples from everyone present to see if we can find a match. It will take a while, but it's the only proper lead I've got."

Lilly could tell this case was vexing Bonnie. There just wasn't enough evidence to form a decent conclusion. There were too many guests to deal with and although the three of them had come up with some primary suspects, it could actually turn out to be someone else entirely. For reasons they weren't aware of yet.

"If there's anything we can do to help, let us know, won't you?" Lilly said, as Bonnie stood up.

"I will. Thank you both. I'll see you later."

Archie and Lilly watched her go, hoping she'd be able to find something relevant soon to set her on the track of the culprit.

Chapter Twelve

FEW MINUTES AFTER Bonnie had left, Lilly and Archie did the same, saying farewell on the pavement outside where Lilly unlocked her bike and Archie sauntered across the road back to the newspaper offices. Just as Lilly was preparing to start her return journey to the shop, her mobile rang. It was Stacey.

"Hi, Stacey, I'm just coming back now. Is everything all right?"

"Yeah, everything's fine. Just letting you know, Bruce called. We left one of our good teacups at his place after the wedding and he said he'd be in today if you wanted to swing by and get it."

"I thought we brought everything back? Was it in the ballroom?"

"No, he said it was in the cellar. Bizarre, huh? Probably someone helping themselves to his wine stash!"

"Wait! Did you say the cellar?"

"Yeah. Why?"

"Stacey, can you do me a favour and ring him back? Tell him I'm on my way. I have to go home and get the car first. I'll be there in about half an hour. Tell him not to touch it."

"Yeah, sure. I'll do it now. Do you think it has something to do with the case?"

"I'm almost sure it does, Stacey."

Just under thirty minutes later, Lilly was pulling up in front of Bruce's home and a moment later, he trudged down the steps to greet her.

"Hello again, Lilly. Your assistant called to tell me you were on your way."

"Hello, Bruce. I didn't get a chance before to say how sorry I am about what happened. How are you doing?"

He stuffed his hands in the pockets of his jeans and shrugged, scuffing the gravel with the toe of his boot. "As well as can be expected. No, actually pretty awful, truth be told. I don't think it has really sunk in yet. It was such a damned shock. I can't understand it. Who would do such a thing? Edmund was a really nice chap. Why would anyone want to even hurt him, let alone kill him?"

Lilly shook her head. "I honestly don't know, Bruce. But I'm sure the police will find out who did it."

"I really hope they do, and soon. It's like the Sword of Damocles hanging over all our heads thinking one of the family or a friend could have done it." He gave a deep sigh. "I hope it was a stranger, you know what I mean?" Lilly nodded. "The alternative is horrible. Anyway, how can I help?"

114

"I believe you've found one of my teacups?"

"Oh, yes, sorry. Come in, I'll get it for you."

"Did Stacey pass on my message about not touching it?"

"She did, unfortunately I'd already put it through the dishwasher."

Lilly groaned. So much for fingerprints. Their first tangible clue and it was already useless.

"I'm sorry, did I do something wrong?" Bruce asked, leading the way down the servants' stairs to the kitchen. "I wouldn't have dreamed of giving it back to you dirty. My mother would have exploded had she known."

"Don't worry, it's not your fault, you weren't to know."

They entered the kitchen, and Lilly spied her teacup on the table. It was one of her good vintage style ones. She had several of the same design she'd brought to the event. But they weren't original pieces, thank goodness, or this one wouldn't have survived the dishwasher. "Can you show me where you found it?" she asked Bruce. "Stacey said it was in the wine cellar?"

"That's right. Goodness knows how it got there. Or why, for that matter? There's no wine down there now, more's the pity. Some of those older vintages command quite a bit of money. I could have sold them to raise funds to keep the place going for a while."

"The teacup was near the fuse box, was it?"

Bruce frowned. "Yes, it was. How did you... oh, no. I'm such an idiot! I can't believe I didn't think of it."

"It's hardly surprising. You've got a lot on your mind," Lilly said. "Let's hope we can find something else that will help."

Bruce nodded, leading her out of a door at the opposite end of the kitchen to the one they'd entered and down a long corridor with an original stone flagged floor. Doors to either side showed what would have been the butler's pantry, laundry room, ironing room, boot room, one that could have been a housekeeper's sitting room and a couple of others Lilly couldn't identify the purpose of. All bare and abandoned now. She supposed there was a similar corridor in the attic, which would have been where servants in days gone by had their sleeping quarters. At the end of the corridor Bruce turned left, pushed opened a large dark oak door set in a shallow alcove, and with the aid of a torch descended the stone stairs behind.

"Can you see all right?" he asked. "I've turned the electricity off at the mains as the lights in the ballroom have been flickering on and off ever since the wedding."

"Yes, I'm fine, as long as you don't go too fast. I thought you'd managed to fix the lights?"

"So did I. There must be damp in the fuse box or something. You can see how far underground we are."

"Has it always been a problem?"

"No, not at all. For a relatively old system, it works remarkably well. Until now, that is. I don't know what to make of it. I suppose at some point I'll have to have the old place rewired, but it'll be a huge expense and there just isn't enough money in the coffers to do it at the moment."

There was no handrail going down to the cellars, so Lilly used the wall as a support. It was rough stone work, cold to the touch but dry as a bone. At the bottom, Bruce told her to stop while he shone the light on the last couple of steps so she didn't fall.

The cellar was a decent size, square, with the left wall given to floor to ceiling shelving to house bottles of wine. Now empty and covered in a thick layer of dust. The opposite wall was free of fixtures until the far end where the fuse box was mounted, and alongside that, an old wooden rack was fixed to the wall on rusty brackets.

"Where did you find the cup?" Lilly asked, following Bruce to the far end of the room.

"Just here, on this shelf," he said, pointing to the rack.

Lilly peered at the shelf and could see a distinct ring shape in the dust. She moved to the fuse box. "Have you opened this since the wedding?"

"No. But actually I didn't open it during the wedding either. I didn't need to as I could see the fuse had just tripped, so I flipped it back on and returned upstairs. I was down here today and about to open it when your assistant called," he said, gesturing to the open toolbox on the floor. "So I went back upstairs to wait for you." He shone his torch to the left of the box, where Lilly saw the main switch for the whole system. "This is where all the power is turned off at once," he explained.

"Okay. Do you have any gloves handy?"

"There are rubber gloves in the kitchen. Will those do?"

Lilly nodded. "Would you mind getting them for me?"

"Will you be okay in the dark for a minute? I'll need the torch."

Lilly said she'd be fine and watched as Bruce bounded up the steps, the small circle of light disappearing the further up he went, until it disappeared completely. Less than a minute later, he was returning, again making short work of the steps. He handed her a pair of bright yellow rubber gloves. She pulled them on and snapped the cuffs.

"Right, let's have a look, shall we?" Lilly carefully depressed the handle and tugged open the metal door, revealing a tangle of wires inside. Bruce shone his torch over her shoulder so she could see. It was immediately apparent what the problem was.

"Look at this," she said. Bruce leaned closer.

"I'll be damned! It's been deliberately cut. But if that happened the night of the wedding, how did the lights come back on when I flipped the fuse switch?"

"I think you were just phenomenally lucky. See here, if I move this half then let go, it bounces back and touches the other half. The wire has been in the same position for years, so it just automatically reverted back to how it was. With the two ends touching, the current was flowing through so the lights would work. The flickering you mention is when one of the pieces moves slightly, breaking the connection, which could be caused by anything. Vibration in the wall, a draft, or even a mouse running across the box."

"So, someone came down here, flipped the ballroom fuse switch to off, opened the door, cut the wire, closed the door then went back upstairs?"

"Yes, I think that's exactly what happened. But for some reason, they had a teacup in their hand on the way down, which they left in their hurry to get away. It was obviously intentional, but the question is, who did it?"

"SHALL I FIX it?" Bruce asked. "I don't want to mess up any more evidence."

"No, we need to leave it for the police to look at. It's possible there will be fingerprints. I'll leave the ballroom fuse switch set to off, but you can turn the main breaker back on. That way you'll still have power to the rest of the house."

With the main lights back on, Bruce switched off the torch. He was leaning against the wine rack, frowning at the fuse box.

"What are you thinking about?" Lilly asked.

"I don't know how they did it without me seeing them. As soon as the lights went out in the ballroom, I dashed down here and got them back on pretty quickly. Could whoever it was really have gone from here, having flipped the switch and cut the wire, and got back to the ballroom in time to stab Edmund in the dark without me passing them?"

"Well, I suppose they must have," Lilly said. "You didn't see anyone, did you?"

"No, but it just doesn't seem plausible. From here to the ballroom there's only one route, and the lights were only off for a few minutes."

"What are you saying, Bruce? You think there was more than one person involved?"

He nodded. "I think there must have been, don't you? One to cut the power and the other to stab Edmund. It's the only way for it to have worked without me seeing anyone."

Lilly stared at him for a second, not really seeing anything, then dragged herself over to the steps and sat on the bottom one, putting her head in her hands. Stupidly, it had never once occurred to her there could be more than one guilty party. But who on earth could they be? She wondered if it had crossed Bonnie's mind? She also wondered if one of Bonnie's officers had been to check the cellar on the night in question? She needed to check.

"Are you all right?" Bruce asked. She'd almost forgotten he was there.

"I'm fine. It's just getting more and more complicated. I need to talk to Bonnie and bring her up to date with what we've found."

"Bonnie? Is that the detective?"

"Yes. She's a friend and is in charge of the investigation. Come on, there's nothing more we can do here."

She got up and turned to go back upstairs, Bruce a little way behind her, when suddenly there was a crunch. She turned back.

"What was that?" she asked.

"I don't know. I trod on something," Bruce replied, lifting his foot.

Lilly jumped back down several steps and walked over to where he was crouching. He'd discovered the source of the noise.

"Cafe de Paris?" Lilly said. Looking questioningly at Bruce, who shrugged.

"It's not mine. I've never seen it before."

"It's a VIP pin. I don't think I've heard of it, have you?"

"Yes, I have. It's a really popular and very famous high-end nightclub in the West End of London. One of the oldest, actually. It opened in the 1920s. It was bombed in the blitz killing staff, band members and diners. It hosts regular cabaret shows every weekend. There's a lot of famous people who have played there."

Lilly nodded. "I have heard of it, actually. I just didn't put two and two together. We'd better leave it in place for the police."

How had it ended up in the cellar unless it was owned by the person who cut the power? If it didn't belong to Bruce and no one else had been down to the cellar, it was more than conceivable they'd just found their first piece of legitimate evidence. And if Bruce's extremely valid reasoning was correct, it could very well belong to the accomplice.

*H*AVING SAID GOODBYE to Bruce, Lilly put the teacup on the passenger seat and sat in her car to call Bonnie. She answered on the third ring.

"Lilly, I'm a bit a busy at the moment. Can I call you back?"

"Actually, it's important, Bonnie. I've found some evidence for the case you need to hear about."

"Okay, hang on," Lilly heard her shout in the background for someone to take over whatever it was she'd been doing. "And make mine a coffee," she added. "Strong and black. Right, I'm back. What is it?"

"Did you send anyone to have a look in the cellar on the night of the wedding?"

"I will have done. Let me check the system." Lilly heard the tapping of a keyboard over the line. "Yes, PC Phipps spoke to the house owner first, who told him the ballroom fuse switch had tripped, so he turned it back on and returned to the ballroom. Phipps went down there and found nothing of any note and could see the switch was back in its correct position, so came back up to the scene. Why?"

Lilly told her about the teacup.

"What? Have you got it?"

"Yes, but it's no good, Bonnie. Bruce had put it through the dishwasher before I got here."

Lilly held the phone away from her ear while her friend ranted and swore like a navvy.

"Is there anything else?" she asked when she came back on the line.

"Yes, we opened the fuse box panel. The wire to the ballroom was deliberately cut."

"Oh, for Pete's sake! Phipps!" she yelled out. "Lilly, I'll call you back," she said and ended the call.

Bonnie called her back ten minutes later, just as she was nearing the junction that would take her into town. She pulled into a lay-by and answered, just as a couple of police vehicles drove by, more than likely heading towards Bruce's.

"Lilly, I've sent some officers back to the scene and will be heading up there myself in a minute. Was there anything else?"

"A couple of things," she replied, and told her about the Cafe de Paris pin and Bruce's suggestion that this must be the work of at least two people because of the timing.

There was a deafening silence and Lilly could almost hear her friend's teeth grinding.

"You know, you're making us look like a bunch of amateurs, don't you?" Bonnie said eventually. "No, actually, worse than amateurs considering you are one. I seriously hope this doesn't get out. My boss will have my guts for garters if it does."

"It's a good job I'm on your side then, isn't it?" Lilly replied. "And don't worry, it won't get out. I won't say anything, and I doubt Bruce will. He just wants this solved as soon as possible. He doesn't care how."

"Don't we all. Right, I better go. Keep in touch, Lilly."

"You too, Bonnie. Let me know if you find anything else."

Chapter Thirteen

THE NEXT DAY, Lilly was back in the shop discussing the recent turn of events with Stacey. Bonnie had telephoned her the previous evening saying her team were going over every inch of the place, inside and out, with a fine-tooth comb, but so far there had only been one other pertinent piece of evidence found. She was furious they had missed the first time.

It was a pair of rubber gloves found buried in the large recycling bin at the side of the house which the public never saw, and it was covered in blood. It had immediately been taken to be tested to see if it was a match for the victim's. Lilly, and everyone else who was aware it had been found, were almost certain it would be. It would explain the lack of fingerprints on the knife, and why blood hadn't been found on any of the suspects present in the ballroom. The existence of the gloves also further indicated that the murder had been premeditated.

"You know, I've been thinking," Stacey said, sipping a peppermint and fig tea blend with obvious pleasure. "Mirac doesn't seem a likely suspect now they've found the gloves and the fact the breaker box was tampered with."

"Why not?"

"Half the reason you thought it could be him was because of his temper tantrum. Yeah, the guy's hot-headed, but that's sort of the opposite of what would be needed in this case, right? It would have to be someone level headed and good at planning and plotting. Not someone who'd go off the deep end for no reason."

Lilly took a break from folding the new sets of napkins, which had just been delivered, and leaned against the counter, looking at her employee proudly. "Very good thinking. You make a valid point, Stacey. He doesn't now seem the type, does he? There was obviously a lot more preparation went into this murder than we initially thought. Which makes the knife being left and the VIP pin dropped in the cellar seem a little sloppy, don't you think?"

Stacey wrinkled her nose while she pondered her reply. "I get the knife being left. I mean, the lights weren't supposed to come back on, were they? It was just sheer luck when the breaker box door was shut, the wires ended up touching. It was supposed to give them enough time to get out of the way, so they didn't look suspicious. And even when the lights came back on, they still managed it. Besides, they were wearing gloves, so they didn't need to go back for it. It didn't point to anyone because there were no fingerprints or anything."

Lilly nodded. "But what about the Cafe de Paris pin? Leaving that was careless. But using gloves, making use of an accomplice, managing to commit a murder and avoid being seen by a room full of people? That takes precision and planning. As well as nerves of steel."

"Yeah, you definitely got two different personalities involved. Whoever cut the electric is definitely not the planner. They left behind evidence as well as failing to keep the power off. But then you've got the actual killer, a total opposite."

"So you think the person who planned all this is the murderer?"

"Yep, looks that way," Stacey said. "And whoever cut the wire was the muscle following orders."

"You'd have thought it would have been the other way round, wouldn't you?" Lilly said. "If you were the brains of the operation, surely you'd get someone else to do the dirty work? I don't know, it seems so personal."

"Well it is. It's someone in the family, right?"

"Mmm, yes, I suppose so."

"Right," Stacey said, hopping off her stool. "I'm starving. What do you want for lunch?"

*L*ILLY HANDED OVER some petty cash to Stacey, and while she was out getting them both something to eat, she put the kettle on for another cuppa. She was humming to herself while going through her selections, trying to choose, when the shop doorbell rang.

She turned with a smile, ready to greet her next customer, and discovered it was James Pepper, Stacey's father. She and James hadn't hit it off at all when they'd first met.

She thought him bombastic and selfish, whereas he'd thought her interfering snoop who was trying to be a parental figure to his daughter. These days they were getting on much better, having decided to set aside their differences and make a concerted effort to get along for the sake of the one person they had in common, Stacey. It was working.

"Hello, James, I didn't know you were in town."

"Good afternoon, Lilly. I've just got off the train," he said, holding up a leather overnight bag. "I came straight here in the hopes of seeing Stacey. Is she out?"

"Yes, she's just popped out to get us both some lunch. She won't be long. Do you want me to call her and add something for you?"

James shook his head. "No, don't worry, I had something on the train."

"How about a cup of tea?"

"Now that I will say yes to, thank you."

"Any preference?"

"Actually, Stacey happened to mention on the phone the other night you'd done a special orange blossom blend recently for a wedding. I rather liked the sound of it. Do you have any left?"

"I do. And you know what; I think I'll join you. I liked it myself."

While Lilly pottered about behind the counter making the tea, she asked James how long he was staying this time?

"Just a few days," he said. "Then I'll have to get back to London. I'd like to stay longer, but it's the best I can do at the moment. However, I was talking to Stacey about her coming to stay with me in London. The benefit of having a student daughter and me being a university lecturer is our holiday times coincide. Do you think you could spare her for a week or so during her autumn break?"

"Of course," Lilly said, serving James his beverage in one of her best teacups. "I think it would do Stacey the world of good to have some time with you in London. She hasn't had much opportunity to travel while she's been here. As long as I get enough notice to make arrangements to cover her hours while she's away, it shouldn't be a problem at all."

"Oh, that's smashing news. Thank you, Lilly."

"Dad! I didn't know you were coming today?" Stacey exclaimed from the door, rushing over to deposit the lunch bags on the counter and give her father a hug.

"I thought I'd surprise you."

"Do you want to share my lunch? Or I could go back and get you something?"

"No, it's fine, Stacey," James said. "Lilly already offered, but I ate on the train."

"I think we should have our lunch here," Lilly said. "It's quiet at the moment."

"Great," Stacey said, taking a stool next to her father and reaching for her sandwich.

"I was just telling Lilly how we'd discussed the possibility of you coming to stay with me in London."

Lilly nodded and smiled at Stacey. "I think it's a great idea. There's so much to do and see in the city, you'll have a fabulous time."

"Hey, yeah! Dad, maybe we could go to Cafe de Paris, do you know it?"

"Cafe de Paris," James said, astonished. "Good grief. How do you know about that?"

Stacey shrugged. "Oh, you know, it just came up recently," Stacey replied, with a quick glance at Lilly. "Have you been there, dad?"

"Believe me, Stacey, you can't live and work in our great capital without going at least once. However, it also happens to be the de facto choice of the faculty for any and all celebrations, so I've been quite a number of times. It's a marvellous place. Like stepping back in time. I was there a few weeks ago, as a matter of fact, for a jazz evening. I rented an authentic vintage tuxedo for the occasion."

"I wish I could have seen that," Stacey said, grinning.

"Well, you're in luck. I happen to have pictures." He reached into his inside jacket pocket for his phone and began scrolling through the various albums. "Ah, here they are. What do you think of those, then?" he said, passing the phone to his daughter. "Your old dad scrubs up quite well, wouldn't you say?"

"Wow, yeah, dad, you look really great," Stacey said as she scrolled through the images. "Did you see anyone famous?"

"Not that night, but in the past there have been a couple of well known pop stars playing when I've been there."

Suddenly, Stacey let out a gasp.

"What is it, Stacey?" Lilly asked.

"Look at this," she said, thrusting the phone at Lilly.

Lilly took one glance at the photo and quickly gave the phone back to Stacey. "Do me a favour, will you, and send me that picture? I need to call Bonnie and Archie immediately."

"Yeah, sure," Stacey said, already tapping the requisite buttons. "Done. It should be on your phone now."

"Thanks, Stacey. I've got to go but I'll be back as soon as I can."

"Goodness, what's happened?" James said. "Where are you rushing off to?"

"A local hostelry. I know who cut the lights in the cellar."

Chapter Fourteen

LILLY SENT A quick text to both Bonnie and Archie with the picture attached, saying she'd meet them both at the Bed & Breakfast asap. She received a thumbs up emoji from Bonnie and a peace sign from Archie, which, despite the reason for meeting them, made her laugh.

She quickly removed the decorations, leaving them tucked up safely outside the shop, swung her leg over her bike and pushed down hard on the pedal. She turned into the B&B car-park, just behind Archie and Bonnie, who'd arrived in separate cars, five minutes later.

Bonnie got out and looked at the others, shaking her head. "You two don't need to be here, you know."

"I'm here for the paper," Archie said. "Especially if you are about to make an arrest."

"Archie, I'm not going to arrest Christopher Rogers. I'm just taking him in for further questioning. All that pin and picture proves is that he's a member of the London club, not that he was in the cellar. The pin could either belong to someone else, or it could be a deliberate plant to lead us in the wrong direction. That's what I intend to find out. If he was there and dropped the pin, then he's obviously the accomplice, but he's not the murderer."

"Well, hopefully he can tell us who is," Lilly said, walking toward the entrance. The others followed.

"I'll go up to the room," Bonnie said. "But I want you both to remain down here, okay?"

Archie and Lilly waited to one side while Bonnie went to speak with the receptionist.

"Do you think Christopher could be working with Yasemin?" Archie asked.

"Yasemin? But they can't stand the sight of one another."

"On the surface, I'd agree with you, but what if it's a ruse? Remember, the only one with blood on them was Yasemin. What if their intention is to split the inheritance? It wouldn't matter then who got the money."

"Crikey, Archie. And you accused me of throwing a spanner in the works?" Lilly said. "To be honest, I have no idea. Maybe the whole family is in cahoots and intends to split the money between them all."

Bonnie had finished speaking with the receptionist and was on the second stair when the young girl screamed. A split second later there was a thud heard from outside. Bonnie vaulted down the steps and charged outside.

"Archie, call an ambulance. Now!"

Lilly dashed outside and skidded to a halt. The inert and twisted body of Christopher Rogers lay on the ground.

"The stupid fool must have jumped when he saw us," Bonnie said. "Lilly, get the first aid kit from my car," she instructed, tossing her the car keys. "Hurry, he's losing a lot of blood."

First aid kit in hand, Lilly ran to Bonnie and crouched down to help. Feeling for a pulse. It was there, but faint. A moment later, Archie joined them.

"The ambulance is on the way. I took the liberty of checking his room. There was no one else there. He definitely jumped. Dear God, what was he thinking? He must have seen us arrive and realised we knew something."

Both of Christopher Rogers' legs were shattered, and one arm, and Lilly could see blood pooling under his head. She grabbed a wad of bandages and held them tight to his skull in an attempt to stem the bleeding. Bonnie was doing the same with one of his legs. The amount of blood loss indicated a probable tear in the femoral artery and Bonnie was tying a tourniquet. Lilly realised if the ambulance didn't arrive soon, they could lose him.

"Archie," Bonnie snapped. "How long for the ambulance?" Archie was just about to answer when they heard the two tone blare of a siren. "Never mind."

A second later, it stopped in the car-park and two paramedics jumped from the back and rushed over. Bonnie, Lilly and Archie stood to one side, leaving the job of stabilising Christopher to the professionals.

"What's his name?" one of them asked.

"Christopher Rogers," Bonnie replied. "He jumped." She turned to Lilly. "I'm going to clean up then I'll follow them to the hospital."

"I'm coming too," Archie said. "Lilly, do you want a lift seeing as though you cycled here?"

Lilly shook her head. "You two go ahead, I'll meet you there."

In the ladies' bathroom, Lilly asked Bonnie if Christopher's room was a crime scene?

"No. It's obvious he jumped of his own accord. I assume you want to snoop around a bit?"

"Of course I do. Is that okay? The B&B will need his room vacant for the next guest anyway, so I thought I'd pack his belongings and bring them to the hospital."

"Yes, all right. But wear gloves. Here," she said, putting a pair of bright blue nitrile gloves on the edge of the sink. "I always carry a spare pair. And photograph everything in situ beforehand, will you? I don't want this coming back to bite me at some point in the future. I'll let the receptionist know you're working with the police on this before I leave. Right, I need to go. I'll see you later at the hospital. Hopefully in the ICU and not the mortuary."

*T*HE YOUNG RECEPTIONIST was in floods of tears behind the desk when Lilly approached. But she had been joined by another member of staff who'd brought her a cup of hot sweet tea.

"I'm sorry you had to witness that," Lilly said.

The girl sniffed. "Thanks. It was just such a shock. I didn't even know him. Will he be all right?"

"I don't know. He's lost a lot of blood, but he was stable by the time he left to go to the hospital. He's in the best place now. I need to collect his belongings do have his room key?"

"It's already open. I gave the man who was with you the spare set so he could check it."

Lilly nodded, thanking her, then went upstairs to room 5b. The door was open when she arrived, the keys still in the lock where Archie had left them, but the room was obviously empty. She snapped on the gloves, took out her phone and entered her first point of call the open window.

Glancing down to the front car-park her stomach gave an involuntary flip. What on earth had possessed him to jump from the window? It must have been guilt for being complicit in the death of his nephew, but as suicide attempts went, it seemed to her to be an almost half-hearted attempt. The B&B was only two storeys high, around twenty five to thirty feet, Lilly estimated. Certainly enough to seriously injure yourself, as had just been proved, but surely not likely to kill yourself outright unless you dived head first?

From the severe damage to his legs and the shoe prints on the window sill, Christopher must have jumped feet first. Then again, with his femoral artery almost severed by a shattered bone, he'd almost succeeded. It had only been the quick thinking of Bonnie that had kept him alive. She wondered if his real intention had been to end his life. Or perhaps it was simply that he wasn't in his right mind and saw it as his only option at the time, hoping it would work. Well, there was only one person who could answer that question. She quickly took photos of the footprints and the drop to the car park below, where the blood was in the process of being hosed away by a member of staff, then closed the window.

She turned her attention to the room itself and decided to start with the chest of drawers. She found Christopher's suitcase on the top shelf of the wardrobe and laid it open on the bed, ready to receive his belongings once she'd searched them thoroughly.

He'd packed lightly for his trip so there wasn't much to check and she mainly found receipts from local cafes and pubs, which she left where they were. She added the box of tea he'd bought from her to the case, then turned her attention to the bathroom. There was nothing there but his black leather wash bag, which she repacked and added to the case. It wasn't until she checked the contents of the wardrobe that she found anything of interest.

The suit he had been wearing to the wedding was hanging from a wooden coat-hanger and the first thing she did was check for signs of blood. There wasn't one single drop to be found, as she'd suspected. He had, in all probability, been in the cellar at the time the murder took place. She checked the left and right pockets but came up empty. The inside pocket, however, revealed a piece of folded paper. It was a note.

Christopher,

Everything is in place. Make sure you cut the power as soon as the first dance starts. No later! Don't mess this up or you'll be sorry.

Well, this certainly proves he cut the power, Lilly thought, although he had been late. The first dance was already over by the time the lights went out. Perhaps, when faced with the fuse box, he'd had second thoughts for a moment? She took the necessary photos for Bonnie, then slipped the note in her pocket and carried on with the search. The only other item of interest she found was in an inside pocket of the suitcase itself. An old, worn photograph of Christopher with two small children, a boy and girl of similar age. She immediately recognised Edmund as a child, so assumed the girl must be his sister Ellie. She had long dark hair, brown eyes and thick glasses. Lilly took the photo to the window to see it better. There was something about the girl that looked familiar, but she couldn't work out what it was. Then again, she saw lots of people every day at the shop and there had been hundreds at the wedding.

Unable to place her, and with time of the essence, she put the photo in her pocket with the note, finished packing, then rang for a taxi to pick her up and take her to the hospital. She'd have to leave her bike for the time being.

Fifteen minutes later, with the receptionist glad to look after her bike for the time being, she was on her way, hoping Christopher Rogers had survived his jump.

Chapter Fifteen

Y THE TIME Lilly got out of the taxi at the hospital, two hours had passed and she arrived to find Bonnie pacing in the waiting area, tanked up on black coffee, looking both exhausted and restless.

"What's happened, Bonnie?"

"He was rushed into theatre as soon as we got here. He's still in there."

"Where's Archie?"

"Gone to get a sandwich from the canteen. What about you? Please tell me you have good news?"

Lilly rolled the small suitcase to a chair and sat down. "Yes, I've found something," she said, but before she could explain, the surgeon appeared, mask dangling from his right hand and a slight sheen of sweat on his forehead.

"Detective?"

"Yes," Bonnie said. "Is he alive?"

"He is. Only thanks to your quick thinking, I might add. We've managed to fix both legs and his arm, but it will be a while before he's able to walk. He'll need a lot of physiotherapy and it's likely he'll have a permanent limp. His head injury was actually less serious than we thought. No brain swelling or intracranial bleeding. Head injuries tend to bleed a lot due to the blood vessels being close to the skin surface. We've stitched him up and he shouldn't have any long-term issues in that regard."

"When can I speak to him?"

"Not until tomorrow at the earliest. He's not come round from the anaesthetic yet and when he does, he'll be on some heavy duty pain killers so probably won't be fully coherent."

"All right, thank you. I'll arrange for one of my officers to be posted outside his room."

"Oh? He's not likely to make a run for it, you know?"

Bonnie smiled. "No, I realise that. Unfortunately, he's part of a serious investigation and there could very well be someone who wants to keep him quiet. It's for his own protection. I'll inform his next of kin but he'll not be allowed any visitors until I've had a chance to talk to him."

The surgeon nodded. "I understand. I'll inform the nurses."

Archie wandered back just as the surgeon left.

"You made it, Lilly," he said with a smile. "So, what's the news from the doctor?"

Bonnie brought him up to date, then went to arrange for an officer to guard Christopher Rogers' room.

"There's not much point in us hanging around here now," Archie said to Lilly.

"There isn't, but Bonnie needs to stop for a bit and eat something. She looks as though she's going to keel over at any moment. If we're not careful, we'll be finding her a spare bed here."

"I agree. What do you suggest?"

"A bit of blackmail. I found something in Christopher's jacket pocket, but I'm only going to share it with her over a decent meal at my place. For the three of us, obviously."

"Very sneaky, Lilly Tweed. But also very clever. Oh, look, she's coming back. I better skedaddle. Lots to do, you know."

"Coward," Lilly whispered with a grin.

It took Lilly five minutes of persuasion for Bonnie to see the sense in what she was saying, and a further two for her friend to admit a bit of down time would be very welcome. Although she was a tad annoyed at Lilly holding the new found evidence to ransom in order to get her to capitulate.

"At the risk of sounding like a cliché, I'm doing it for your own good, Bonnie. You're my friend and I can see you're making yourself ill over this case. I'm not withholding anything from you, just delaying it a bit to feed you so you can get your strength back and your brain firing on all cylinders again. I don't cook for just anyone you know."

"I know you don't," Bonnie said, giving her friend a quick hug. "Okay, let me just call the station.

"I need to call Stacey too. I've left her running the shop on her own for the umpteenth time. I really must see about getting some new staff."

As Lilly expected, Stacey was fine and had managed the shop with no problems. It had been quite busy since Lilly had left, but she'd roped James in to help her, and Fred had turned up a couple of hours later to lend a hand as well. Lilly apologised for once again, leaving her in the lurch and promised to put an advert in the paper for a job vacancy.

Stacey had been shocked to learn of Christopher's jump from the window and told Lilly she'd lock up the shop and keep Earl overnight so she could do what she needed to. It was pointless her coming back as it would be closing time soon, anyway. Lilly thanked her and said she'd be in bright and early in the morning, allowing the girl a well-deserved lie in. But it was likely she'd have to go to the hospital later in the day to talk to Christopher Rogers with Bonnie and Archie.

"Hey, don't worry, it's fine," Stacey said. "You just go and solve the case."

Lilly ended the call, wondering if she could.

$\mathcal{B}$ACK AT HER cottage that evening, after a starter of soup with crusty bread, followed by lasagna with an Italian chopped salad, Archie, Bonnie and herself discussed the case. Starting with the note Lilly had found in Christopher's jacket pocket.

"So, that definitely confirms he was the one in the cellar and cut the power," Bonnie said, reading the note. "And if I'm right," she added, scrolling through the photos on her phone and finding the one she wanted. "And I am," she said, showing them the image. "The handwriting matches the note found in Edmund's pocket."

"Yes, it's definitely the same hand," Archie confirmed. "A south paw too by the looks of it."

"How do you know?" Bonnie asked.

"I might not be a graphologist, my dear detective, but I am a writer. The direction the letters slant for one thing, particularly the stroke over the letter i's."

"Does the fact it's a stroke rather than a dot mean anything, Archie?" Lilly asked, pouring them all a cup of tea.

"That's beyond my limited knowledge, I'm afraid. It could be something as simple as the fact it was written in a rush, or more complicated. For example;, they are a psychopath who doesn't play well with others and will only eat beef on Tuesdays."

Bonnie snorted. "Thanks for that, Archie. Very helpful. But, you think whoever wrote this is left handed?"

"No, I think they wrote it with their left hand. It could be a deliberate attempt to disguise their writing."

"Great. So we're either looking for a left-handed writer, a right-handed writer writing with their left hand, or someone ambidextrous?"

"That about sums it up," Archie said, nodding. "But there can't be too many that are ambidextrous within your suspect pool. And I think either that or a left hander is more likely. It's very neat writing."

"Okay. I'll just have to ask them all to give us handwriting samples. It was a good find, Lilly, thank you. Was there anything else?"

"I've sent you all the photos I took, but I also found this in Christopher's suitcase. It's a photo of him with Edmund and I presume Ellie." She handed the photo to Bonnie.

Bonnie pondered it for a while. "I'm not sure how it helps us with the case, apart from to show they used to all be on good terms. But thanks Lilly," she said again, handing the photo back.

"I thought she looked familiar," Lilly said.

"She looks a bit like her brother."

"Yes, that's probably it. Do you know if Edmund actually went to meet the person who wrote the note to him?"

Bonnie shook her head. "Not at the moment. He obviously met Yasemin in the garden, you were there, but I can't find anyone who can corroborate him meeting anyone else either before or after the ceremony."

"Perhaps with his bride-to-be having second thoughts, he never made that meeting?" Archie suggested.

"Yes, that's also possible."

"So, have we done with work for this evening?" Archie asked.

"I don't think there's any more we can do now," Bonnie said. "What about you, Lilly?"

"Personally, I think we switch off completely. I have ice cream."

"That certainly clinches the deal for me," Archie said. And Bonnie agreed.

The three old friends spent the next couple of hours chatting and generally winding down, discussing anything and everything except the case. Lilly could see it was doing Bonnie the world of good and she was pleased as well as relieved. But at the back of her mind, she was still trying to wrestle with the image in the photograph. Because she was sure that whoever that young girl had grown up to be, she'd seen the woman recently.

Chapter Sixteen

THE NEXT MORNING Lilly arrived early as she'd promised, having walked through the park to The Wharf B&B to pick up her bike, and got everything ready for the day ahead. She was just unlocking the front door, ready to open, when Stacey arrived with Earl.

"Morning, Lilly."

"Good morning, Stacey. Thanks again for yesterday. I hope your dad didn't mind helping out? It was very kind of him."

"No problem, and dad enjoyed himself. I think he liked us doing something together, you know? And he was a big hit with all the ladies. So how is Christopher Rogers? I can't believe he did that."

"He was stable when we left the hospital yesterday, but he's got a long road to recovery. I'm waiting to hear from Bonnie as to when we can talk to him. Now we know he was the one who cut the power we need to know who he was working with."

Stacey nodded. "Yeah, the murderer. I wonder who it is?"

"At this moment I honestly have no idea, Stacey."

"I hope you find out soon. Shall I make some tea before the first customers arrive?"

"Good idea. You choose."

The morning flew by as they were kept busy with a constant stream of customers. At twelve-thirty, Stacey dashed out to buy their lunch, which they took turns to eat in the storeroom kitchen at the back of the shop. The afternoon slowed down a little thankfully as Lilly received a text from Bonnie at two o'clock. Christopher Rogers was awake. Archie turned up five minutes later.

"I've come to give you a lift to the hospital, Lilly, if you want to go?"

"I do. Thanks, Archie," she said, then turned to Stacey. "Have you got hold of Fred? Is he able to come and help?"

Stacey nodded. "Yep, he'll be here in about ten minutes."

"That's a relief. Can you pay him from the till and leave a note of the amount? And do thank him for me, Stacey. I don't know what I'd do without him to call on at a moment's notice."

"Will do. Good luck at the hospital."

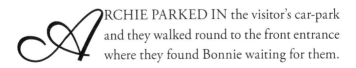

RCHIE PARKED IN the visitor's car-park and they walked round to the front entrance where they found Bonnie waiting for them.

On the way to the room, Bonnie outlined her plan. "Obviously I will be asking the questions, but if there's anything either of you think I've missed, then ask. Archie, I'm happy for you to take notes, but I want to see anything you intend to put in the paper prior to publication. Although at the moment, I don't know when that will be. All right?"

"Of course."

"One of my officers will also be present, taking down Christopher Rogers' official statement. I'll get him to sign that once we've finished. Do either of you have any questions?"

Both Lilly and Archie shook their heads. They walked the rest of the way in silence. Outside the room, they found a police constable waiting, notebook in hand, chatting to the colleague who'd been posted to guard Christopher's room. Bonnie had a quick word with them both while Lilly and Archie waited, then all four of them entered.

Lilly had to stop herself from gasping when she saw the bed. There was hardly anything of the man that wasn't bandaged or in a cast. Both legs were in plaster from ankle to hip, his arm was also in both a cast and a sling. And his head was completely bandaged, showing only a face covered in a plethora of cuts and a rainbow of bruises. He was also on a drip, *for fluids and painkillers as needed*, Lilly thought. He groaned slightly and opened his eyes as he heard them enter.

Bonnie made the introductions and informed him of his rights. Once he confirmed he had understood what she'd said to him, Bonnie took a seat by the side of his bed. Lilly chose the one on the other side of the bed, and Archie and the police constable sat on chairs against the wall, out of Christopher Rogers' line of sight.

Bonnie began by asking how he was feeling?

"How do you think?" he replied in a weak, raspy voice.

"I have some questions regarding the murder of your nephew Edmund Rogers," Bonnie began. "Evidence has recently come to light placing you in the cellar of Bruce Rogers' home on the night in question. We know you were responsible for cutting the power to the ballroom. However, I would like to know how you got back to the ballroom so quickly and without anyone seeing you in order to commit the murder?"

"It wasn't me! I didn't kill Edmund. I didn't know they were going to kill him. You must believe me."

"Who are they, Christopher? Who were you working with?"

He closed his eyes and Lilly watched as a tear tracked down his cheek. "I don't know," he whispered.

"What do you mean, you don't know? I don't understand. Someone you don't know asked you to cut the ballroom lights, and you just did it? Why on earth would you do that, Christopher?"

"Because they said they could get me my rightful inheritance. They wanted thirty percent when I got it and all I had to do was make sure the power went out when they said."

Bonnie got up and started to pace, shaking her head. She turned back. "You better start again from the beginning. When and how did they contact you?"

"WATER," HE SAID.

Lilly grabbed the plastic mug on the bed-side cabinet and held the straw to his lips while he drank. He nodded his thanks, then spoke.

"It was about a month ago. I got an anonymous letter."

"Where? At your home in London?" Bonnie asked.

"Yes. They said they had found a way to get me the inheritance, but they expected a share once it came into my hands. Thirty percent like I said before. I agreed and..."

"How did you agree?" Bonnie interrupted. "How did you make contact?"

"It was a post office box in London. I can't remember it."

Bonnie sighed. "Do you have it written down anywhere?"

"No. He told me to burn everything once I'd replied. I got another letter the week before the wedding with instruc-tions. Cut the power when the first dance started. On the day itself, a note was slipped into my pocket reminding me what to do. I was a bit late, but I did it. They said I'd be sorry if I didn't. I knew the fuse box was in the cellar."

"How? Did the anonymous note writer tell you this?"

"Yes." Bonnie glanced at Lilly and raised an eyebrow. It must be someone who knew the house, then turned her attention back to Christopher.

"All right, go on."

"I cut the lights then went back up to the ballroom..."

"Wait. Why weren't you seen by Bruce when he went to the cellar to try to get the lights back on?"

"I hid in the kitchen until he'd gone. I used the torch on my phone and hurried back to the ballroom. When the lights came back on... Edmund was dead," Christopher gulped and began to sob.

Bonnie turned to Lilly. "Why didn't any of the kitchen staff see him?"

"They were all upstairs clearing the tables and watching the first dance. The kitchen was empty."

"Christopher, stop crying. What did you expect would happen when you turned the lights out? Surely you realised it would be something like this?"

"No!" he wailed. "I didn't know what the plan was. Do you think I'd have gone through with it if I'd known? I just did as I was told. I was stupid and greedy. I just wanted my money. I... I didn't know they'd kill him."

Archie muttered 'idiot' under his breath and got a sharp look from Bonnie. Christopher didn't seem to hear.

"Are you getting all this, Simpson?" Bonnie asked the constable. Lilly had almost forgotten he was there.

"Yes, Ma'am."

"All right, Christopher," she said. "What happened next?"

"Nothing. Everything went quiet. No more letters. I thought whoever it was had some plan to stop Yasemin from getting the money but I haven't heard anything. So I called my solicitor. He called me back yesterday morning."

"And what did he say?"

Christopher sighed deeply and closed his eyes. "It's over. Ellie's back."

"*W*HAT?" LILLY BLURTED out in surprise. "Edmund's sister has returned?"

"She's going to get everything," Christopher said. "She must have read about Edmund in the paper."

Lilly turned to look at Archie, who shook his head. She knew he hadn't printed anything in the Plumpton Mallet Gazette, but Bonnie had also tasked him with ensuring the murder wasn't reported elsewhere. He'd pulled in a lot of favours within his network and made a fair few promises. So far, he'd been successful. Plus, she knew those way higher than Bonnie in the police hierarchy had also put a temporary gag order on the press. It had worked so far, but it was only a matter of time before the story broke among cries of 'freedom of speech' and 'the public has a right to know.' They had to solve this case and quickly. Christopher Rogers was their best option.

"It hasn't been in any of the papers," Bonnie said.

"Well, I don't know how she found out then. Nobody in the family has heard from her. But she has. And she's ruined everything."

"And this was the reason you jumped?" Bonnie asked.

"What do you think? I helped to kill my nephew, then found out it was all for nothing. I'm ruined."

He sank back on his pillow, utterly exhausted and grey with pain. Bonnie indicated it was time to leave. They'd got as much as they were going to out of Christopher Rogers today.

Outside the room, she told Simpson to go back to the station and type up his notes and to find someone to relieve the constable who was still guarding the door. Lilly saw her send a quick email before she turned back to them.

"Surely you don't believe all that guff, do you, Bonnie?" Archie asked as the three of them walked down the stairs. "That he was just following orders from some anonymous source via letter, of all things, just for a bit of cash?"

"Actually, as stupid as his actions were, I believe he's telling the truth. It's not just a bit of cash, Archie. When you take into account the property, jewellery, various investments and cash, it amounts to something north of four million pounds."

"Crikey!" Archie said. "I stand corrected. I had no idea it was that much."

"It looks like we've found our motive," Lilly said. "But you heard what Christopher said, Ellie's back, and she's the obvious suspect now, wouldn't you say?"

"But she wasn't at the wedding," Archie said.

"No," Bonnie said. "But if she talked Christopher into cutting the lights, then it's more than feasible she managed to persuade some other poor sap to stab Edmund. Now, I need to get to the mortuary. I want to compare the two notes we found just to confirm they match."

"I'll come with you," Lilly said.

They both looked at Archie, who raised his hands, palms out, as if warding off an unseen force. "As much as I appreciate that fabulous invitation, ladies, I must get back to the office. Bonnie, on a more serious note, if you learn anything new and can share, could you give me a call?"

"Of course, but don't hold your breath, Archie. It's still an open case and you already know far more than you're supposed to."

151

*A*S ARCHIE DISAPPEARED out of the hospital's exit, Lilly and Bonnie continued down the stairs to the basement area and the mortuary.

"I can't believe how convoluted this case is getting," Bonnie said as they trudged down the third flight of stairs. "But hearing Ellie is back on the scene certainly changes things."

"I was thinking the same. You're going to get in touch with the solicitor to see what they say about their contact with Ellie, I assume?"

"I sent an email when we came out of Christopher's room. I'm waiting for a reply and I'll be going there next."

Lilly smiled. "You're a good detective, Bonnie."

"I'm still a beginner, Lilly. And believe me, I feel it more than ever with this investigation."

Lilly had never been to the mortuary and didn't really know what to expect. As they pushed through a set of double doors painted in a dull green with a port hole in each, she found herself in a well-lit corridor. Albeit one which smelled of disinfectant, overlaid with something she didn't want to guess at.

Bonnie led her to the far end where there was an office and knocked on the open door. The middle aged man in the white coat turned surprised at first. Visitors were few and far between in his domain, particularly ones who walked in and knocked on the door, then he smiled when he saw Bonnie.

"Have you come for my report, Bonnie?"

"Actually, I just wanted to double check the note found in the victim's pocket, but I'll take it if it's ready."

"It is. I'll get it and bring it to the evidence room. The note is there still," he said, looking at Lilly over the top of his spectacles.

"Sorry," Bonnie said, "This is Lilly Tweed. Lilly, this is Doctor Perry."

"Ah, of course," he said. "I recognise you. I get my teas at your shop occasionally."

Lilly smiled. "I thought you looked familiar. Let me see, hibiscus and rooibos, I think?"

He nodded. "You've a very good memory. I must get some more actually while I think about it. Now, if you want to go ahead, I'll find my report."

A couple of doors back up the hall on the opposite side of the corridor, Bonnie opened a door. It led to a small room with racks of stainless steel shelving on which were a series of large black plastic storage boxes. Each one had a piece of card with a name on taped to the front. Bonnie found the one for Edmund Rogers and brought it to the central table. She put on her gloves and lifted out the note, comparing it to the one found in Christopher's jacket pocket.

"There is absolutely no doubt these were written by the same person," she said, showing them to Lilly.

"So now we know the same person who convinced Christopher to cut the power is the same one who wanted to meet Edmund in the garden before the ceremony," Lilly said.

Doctor Perry entered then and handed Bonnie his full autopsy report.

"Any surprise findings?" she asked.

"No, it was as we expected. The knife severed his carotid artery, and he was rendered unconscious very quickly and died not long after."

Bonnie continued reading the report while Lilly was studying the notes.

"He had a tattoo?"

"Yes, inside his right arm. Odd design. I didn't know what to make of it, but thought it looked like a wave."

Lilly spun round. "What? What did you say?"

"Lilly, what is it?" Bonnie asked.

"Can I see it? The tattoo?"

"Yes, of course," Doctor Perry said, taking the report from Bonnie and turning to the back. "The photographs are in here." He thumbed through until he found the right page, then laid it on the table for Bonnie and Lilly to study.

Lilly gasped. "I don't believe it!"

"What is it, Lilly?" Bonnie asked again in frustration.

"Wait a minute," she pulled the photograph out of her pocket and, after staring at it a minute, thrust it under Bonnie's nose. "Look at this. Now, imagine this girl all grown up. Take away the glasses and make them blue contact lenses, dye her hair blond and imagine she's had a nose job."

Bonnie laughed and stared incredulously at her friend. "That's a lot of imagining you're asking for, Lilly."

"Please, Bonnie, just try."

Bonnie took the picture with the intention of humouring her friend, then it suddenly dawned on her who she was looking at. "Oh, my god."

"You see it too, don't you?" Lilly said.

"Yes. Come on. We've got to go."

They rushed out of the mortuary, with Bonnie shouting her thanks to Doctor Perry over her shoulder. She had an arrest to make.

Chapter Seventeen

AT THE CAR Bonnie took a quick minute to send an urgent email to the solicitors dealing with the inheritance money from Christopher's parents, then jumped in the car, urging Lilly to do the same. Once inside, she made a call to the station and arranged for an officer to be posted at the rear of the premises in case their suspect decided to try and make a run for it. She also arranged for a plainclothes officer inside. "And make sure you get a table near the door just in case," she finished.

"Here," she said to Lilly. "Take my phone. If the solicitor emails back, open it and read it to me. I want confirmation we're pursuing the right individual before we go in all guns blazing to make an arrest."

"Of course. But we know it's her, Bonnie," Lilly replied.

"I know. I'm ninety-nine percent sure, but it's that final one percent which could cost me my job if we're wrong."

"Would you mind if I let Archie know, Bonnie?"

"No, go ahead. I promised he'd be the first to know when we had the murderer. The exclusive is his. He deserves it. Just make sure you tell him not to give the game away if he pays her a visit. Better still, ask him to wait somewhere out of sight until he sees us go in, would you?"

Lilly made the call and once she'd told Archie the name of the person they were certain had killed Edmund, even Bonnie could hear his screech of, "What? I don't believe it!"

"Imagine how I feel, Archie," Lilly said. "I have been managed and played right from the start."

There were a couple more minutes of conversation then Lilly ended the call. A second later Bonnie's phone pinged, signifying an email. Lilly opened it.

"It's from the solicitor. He's attached the full copy of the will, including the signature. We are right, Bonnie," she said, turning the screen so her friend could see.

"Ellie Elizabeth Roman. So she did change her surname name officially then?"

"Yes. According to the solicitor she changed it several years ago, presumably when she disappeared, but has all the necessary documents to prove it. She chose to go by a short-ened version of her middle name. Bethany. Edmund's very own sister is the one who killed him, Bonnie."

"**W**HAT DO YOU mean when you said to Archie you'd been managed?" Bonnie asked, as she turned onto the road leading into Plumpton mallet.

Lilly explained how thrilled she'd been when Stacey told her they'd been asked to cater for Edmund and Yasemin's wedding, but with the food side not being her forte she'd obviously had to find someone to go into partnership with and had chosen Bethany. Or so she'd thought.

"She was really clever about it, too. First there was a flier put through my shop door advertising catering for various celebrations, weddings being at the top of the list. Then I'd popped round to get lunch for Stacey and me one day and there was a wedding cake on prime display in the cafe window. And of course her own fliers and a poster by the till, as well as a smaller one on each table, advertising wedding catering. It's hardly surprising she was the first one I thought of when I needed a partner, is it?"

"Blimey, Lilly, that's a bit spooky. Are you sure?"

"Absolutely. It was like some sort of subliminal messaging drilled into my brain. It worked too. I'm furious I've been played so easily."

"Well, if it's any compensation, she's about to get her comeuppance. We're here."

Bonnie had parked in the town car park at the rear of the row of buildings where both Lilly's tea shop and Bethany's cafe were situated, so it was only a minute walk round the corner to the front. On the way past the back door, Bonnie nodded briefly to the police constable, who was situated outside and ready for action should there be any.

Inside, they found Bethany poring over some paperwork at the nearest table to the counter. A casually dressed young man at a table near the door looked up when they entered, but ignored them and went back to his paper. Lilly recognised him as one of Bonnie's team, though. She also spied Archie outside the window, about to enter.

Bethany looked up as they approached. "Hello, Lilly, Bonnie," she said. "Sorry about the mess. I've been inundated with catering enquiries since the wedding. Have a seat and I'll get you both a coffee," she said, standing and moving toward the counter.

Clearly Bethany had no idea she'd been caught. Even with the detective leading the investigation into her brother's murder standing right in front of her.

"No coffee for me," Lilly said. "Bonnie?"

"None for me either."

"No problem," Bethany said. "Oh, Lilly, I don't suppose you've transferred my share of the catering money over, have you?" she asked, closing the small gate and dropping the counter in place, before positioning herself behind the till.

"I haven't had time yet. But why do you need it?"

"What do you mean? I earned it."

"But aren't you about to get your inheritance? I understand it's in the millions, Bethany. Or should I say, Ellie?"

The next few seconds were a complete blur for Lilly as Bethany, aka Ellie, dashed along the counter and through a back door, Bonnie cried 'get her!' and vaulted over the counter in pursuit and the young constable followed her, sailing over the counter like an Olympian and disappearing through the door behind his boss.

Lilly stood rooted to the spot in shock and nearly jumped out of her skin when a hand touched her shoulder.

"Come on, she's gone out the back way," Archie said, grabbing her hand and pulling her outside and round the block.

They found Bethany face down on the pavement being handcuffed by a very pleased constable, while Bonnie read her her rights and formally arrested her for the murder of Edmund Rogers.

Chapter Eighteen

A COUPLE OF DAYS after the arrest, an hour before they were due to open, Lilly and Stacey found themselves entertaining Archie and Bonnie at The Tea Emporium while Bonnie brought them up to date with the case.

"But why did she do it?" Stacey asked, pouring the tea. "I mean, her own brother? I don't get it."

"Because, according to her, she lost the love of her life due to her family's inherent racism," Bonnie said. "They were engaged to be married, although they hadn't told either of their families, when he upped and left her because of how he was treated. Most of them, as you know, were quite vocal about how wrong he was for her and although Edmund didn't actually voice out loud, his disappointment in who she'd chosen, he certainly didn't stand up for her either."

"So, she killed him because he didn't stick up for her?" Stacey asked, aghast.

"It was part of it, although not the main reason," Bonnie said. "But the way he acted, in her eyes, was the cruelest blow of all. And to quote her, 'My own brother, with whom I've been through so much and was so close to, sided with the family, not me.' So she left and reinvented herself. Successfully too. But she never let go of her hatred for them all."

"So, she's been planning this for years?" Archie asked, pen poised over his notebook.

He'd already written the account of the murder and the subsequent arrest of the victim's estranged sister, now masquerading as a caterer who provided the food for the ill-fated wedding. It was a reporter's dream story and had made the front page news of the Plumpton Mallet Gazette, as well as being syndicated to the nationals. It was sensational stuff and Archie was being talked about in glowing terms. It was probable that he would be nominated for a Press Award.

Now, he was looking for the finer details in order to produce a series of more in-depth articles, a deep dive into the backgrounds of the players, is how he'd put it when he'd talked to Lilly.

Bonnie shook her head and took a sip of her tea. "No, actually, surprisingly enough. It was only when she read the announcement of Edmund's engagement to Yasemin that she saw red at his hypocrisy and started to plan. The money from the inheritance was just a bonus, not the motive. You were right about her 'managing' you, by the way, Lilly."

"I thought I was. She admitted it, did she?"

"Yes, I asked her about it and she said it was just as you'd described. She was very smug about how easy it had been to push you in the direction she wanted. Don't worry, I soon brought her down to size," Bonnie added, when she saw how upset and angry Lilly was getting.

"Lilly, it's how adverts work, you know?" Archie said. "Any one of us would have done the same thing in your position. You're bombarded with the same image and message repeated over and over on television, the radio or in newspapers and magazines, and eventually you end up buying whatever it is they're selling because it's been implanted in your brain. It happens to millions every day; don't beat yourself up about it."

Lilly smiled at Archie and squeezed his arm. "Thank you, Archie. I needed to hear that. You're right, of course. It still infuriates me though."

Archie gave her a smile and a wink before turning back to Bonnie. "So, how did she actually do it, Bonnie? I obviously need to get the facts straight for the paper. Can you go through it for me?"

"Yes, Archie, I will. Okay, this is what she said..."

ACCORDING TO BONNIE, Bethany had seen the announcement of the forthcoming marriage between her brother and Yasemin in the paper. Initially, it had not been her intention to have anything more to do with her family. In fact, it had been years since she had seen or heard from any of them. She'd hardly given them a second thought since running away as a young girl. But the reasons she'd had to leave, as well as the loss of the man she loved, had always been at the back of her mind.

The fact her brother was going to marry a Turkish girl had incensed her, and she realised she'd never got over what had happened. Her hatred was deep rooted, buried, but suddenly came rushing to the front of her mind in an explosion of anger. This was the final straw, and she began to put a plan into action that would get rid of the brother she felt had failed her, while simultaneously laying the blame at the feet of the uncle she hated. She fully expected Christopher Rogers to be arrested as an accomplice if not the perpetrator and hoped the police would pick one of the family, preferably Rachel, as being his partner.

Bruce's house was already familiar to her as it had belonged to a distant cousin previously, and she'd visited as a child twice. She thought she knew where the fuse box was located, but to be absolutely sure, she took the opportunity during the rehearsal dinner to double check and work out the plan in more detail. Lilly realised Bethany had never once set foot in the breakfast room while the guests were there. Choosing to send the courses up and down the dumb waiter. She couldn't risk being recognised.

On the day of the wedding, she'd sent Edmund a note asking him to meet her in the rose garden, her intention to tell him who she was and enact a happy reconciliation. But swearing him to secrecy because she didn't want the rest of the family to know who she was. Her reasoning was to get him off guard, so when she approached him in the dark during the first dance, he wouldn't cry out in surprise, but so he would know it was her.

But, due to the wobble that Yasemin had had about Edmund's debt, he never went to the rose garden to meet the note writer, staying with Yasemin instead. By the time he and Yasemin left, having made up, it was too late.

Christopher Rogers' part in the plan was already known by all of them, so when he cut the lights it was Bethany's turn. She was already upstairs clearing the tables, and she made sure all the staff were absent from the kitchen in order for Christopher to do his part without being seen. Once the lights went out, she'd already positioned herself close to the couple and managed to separate Edmund, stab him and then get back to the table without anyone being any the wiser. She was wearing rubber gloves, but as she was in charge of catering and clearing tables at the time, no one thought it out of place. But she knew no one would look twice at a member of the staff, anyway.

When the lights came back on and Yasemin screamed, everyone automatically looked at the dance floor. While their attention was held elsewhere, Bethany took off her gloves and hid them in the crockery she was collecting from the tables, then took it all to the kitchen. She disposed of the gloves in the bins, then returned to the kitchen and ran the dishwasher. Any blood that had transferred to the china was immediately washed away.

"She did say in hindsight she should have thrown the gloves in the dishwasher at the same time. She admitted that was a stupid mistake, but was still running on adrenaline, having just killed her brother. She wasn't thinking straight, just enacting, exactly, the plan that she'd already formulated and convinced herself would work. She didn't dare deviate from it in case she made an error."

"Well, thank heavens she didn't wash the gloves," Archie said, scribbling furiously.

"She told us in the kitchen about Edmund having a sister," Stacey said. "She said Bruce had told her, but obviously that was a lie, right?"

"It was. I spoke with Bruce and he told me they had never had a conversation at all. It was purely to misdirect the investigation away from her."

"Why didn't she have any blood on her?" Archie asked.

"Because she was wearing a plastic apron," Lilly said. "I've just remembered. It's obvious when you realise. It looks perfectly normal for a caterer. Who would give it a second thought?"

"Mmm. It makes sense, I suppose," Archie said. "But she was shorter than Edmund and stabbed him in the neck. Surely the blood would have gone on her shoulders? I mean her clothes rather than the apron?"

Everyone looked at Bonnie for an answer.

"Very astute of you, Archie Brown. Yes, you would be right in thinking that, expect she grabbed his arm and pulled him down, whispering in his ear who she was. It was enough of a shock to him that he didn't put up a fight. She then stabbed him from the side. What blood there was hit the apron she was wearing. She pulled out the knife and dropped it as Edmund fell. She had the luck of the devil that night."

"Devil is the perfect word," Archie said.

"So what, she took the apron off at the same time as the gloves and hid that too?" Stacey asked.

Bonnie nodded.

"Did you find the apron?" Lilly asked.

"Eventually. It was wrapping a side of beef in the freezer. Totally camouflaging the blood."

"Wow," Stacey said. "She thought of everything."

"Well, not everything," Lilly said. "We did catch her after all."

Chapter Nineteen

*I*T HAD BEEN a couple of weeks since the murder of Edmund Rogers and the arrest and charge of both his sister and his Uncle Christopher. Lilly and Stacey had returned to normality, although Stacey had cut back on her hours in the tea shop now her autumn term at college had started.

On this particular day, they were seated at the counter drinking tea while Lilly was preparing to share with the girl exciting new plans for the future of the shop. Earl was snuggled in Stacey's lap while she was skimming the morning paper.

"Archie's last article on the case was really good. It's no wonder he's going to get an award."

"He deserves it. I'm really pleased for him. Oh, by the way, it looks as though Yasemin is set to receive Edmund's inheritance. It means she can pay off his debt."

"Hey, that's good news. I was wondering if you'd heard from her. So Bethany, or Ellie, or whatever we're calling her, doesn't get a dime? Sorry, a penny I mean?"

Lilly shook her head. "Apparently there is a law called The Forfeiture Law which prevents a criminal from benefitting from their crime in any way. Apparently it was established primarily to prevent convicted murderers from being able to inherit from their victim's estate."

"So she gets nothing?"

"Nothing but a life sentence in prison."

"Yeah, well, she deserves it. What about Christopher?"

"He's obviously facing charges as well as her accomplice, but Bethany has sworn he had no idea what her ultimate plan was."

"Seriously?" Stacey said.

"Hard to believe, isn't it? As my mum used to say, 'He hasn't the brains he was born with.' But he's still got a long way to go before he'll be able to leave hospital, anyway."

"I'm glad it's over. Score another one for Lilly Tweed, exceptional sleuth! You should start putting that on your business cards. So, you said you had some news?"

"I do. I've made a big decision this week, and it's going to impact The Tea Emporium."

"Oh, gosh, what?"

"You may not know, but Bethany actually leased the premises for the cafe. With everything that has happened, the owner put it up for sale privately. And I bought it, well half of it."

"You bought our favourite cafe!" Stacey cried in excitement. "Really?"

"I did. My little teashop is expanding. We'll now have both locations, and of course the cafe will be adding my teas to their menu. I know you're going to have to cut back your hours because of college, so I thought I could train some of the cafe staff to work here as well. We can make it so they are flexible and can work between the two."

"That's awesome," Stacey said, eyes shining with excitement.

"It means we will be hiring new employees and, if you want to, I'd be delighted if you could oversee the scheduling. You have superb organisation skills, Stacey, and I'd love it if you could run that side of things. It would naturally be a promotion and with added remuneration. You don't have to make a decision straightaway. But if you could think about it?"

Stacey looked away for a second. "Okay, I've thought about it and my answer is yes! Wow, this is really exciting, Lilly."

"I think so, too. But remember me saying I'd only bought half of the cafe? Well, we do have someone new we will be working with who bought the other half."

"Oh?"

"Yes. I couldn't risk investing the whole amount, it was a bit too much. So, I reached out to someone I knew who was looking for a career change."

Right on cue, the shop door opened and a familiar face entered. The smirk on Lilly's face obviously gave her away.

"No," Stacey muttered under her breath. "You must be kidding."

"Hello, Lilly, Stacey," Abigail Douglas said, smiling as she approached them. She looked a lot better than when Lilly had last seen her. "I'm so excited to start this new venture with you both."

"We're going to be working together, then?" Stacey asked.

"That's right," Lilly said. "So, ladies, shall we get started?"

Lilly looked between Stacey and Abigail with a huge grin plastered on her face and metaphorically rolled up her sleeves. Let the next adventure begin.

If you enjoyed *A Bitter Bouquet*, the fourth book in the Tea & Sympathy series, please leave a review on Amazon. It really does help other readers find the books.

ABOUT THE AUTHOR

J. New is the author of *THE YELLOW COTTAGE VINTAGE MYSTERIES*, traditional English whodunits with a twist, set in the 1930's. Known for their clever humour as well as the interesting slant on the traditional murder mystery, they have all achieved Bestseller status on Amazon.

J. New also writes two contemporary cozy crime series:

THE TEA & SYMPATHY series featuring Lilly Tweed, former newspaper Agony Aunt now purveyor of fine teas at The Tea Emporium in the small English market town of Plumpton Mallet. Along with a regular cast of characters, including Earl Grey the shop cat.

THE FINCH & FISCHER series featuring mobile librarian Penny Finch and her rescue dog Fischer. Follow them as they dig up clues and sniff out red herrings in the six villages and hamlets that make up Hampsworthy Downs.

Jacquie was born in West Yorkshire, England. She studied art and design and after qualifying began work as an interior designer, moving onto fine art restoration and animal portraiture before making the decision to pursue her lifelong ambition to write. She now writes full time and lives with her partner of twenty-two years, two dogs and five cats, all of whom she rescued.

If you would like to be kept up to date with new releases from J. New, you can sign up to her *Reader's Group* on her website www.jnewwrites.com where you will also receive a link to download the free e-book, *The Yellow Cottage Mystery*, the short-story prequel to The Yellow Cottage Vintage Mystery series.

Printed in Great Britain
by Amazon